BLOODY PULP

Also by Mike Attebery
On/Off – A Jekyll and Hyde Story
Billionaires, Bullets, Exploding Monkeys
Seattle On Ice

BLOODY PULP

by
Mike Attebery

Cryptic Bindings
Seattle, Washington

Cryptic Bindings
Seattle, Washington
Bloody Pulp

Cryptic Bindings
Visit our website at www.crypticbindings.com
Read Mike Attebery's Blog: www.mikeattebery.com

First Edition: November 2012

ISBN: 978-0-615-68587-8

Printed in the United States of America.

for Steph

A murder of crows leapt from the snow-covered branches that hung heavy over the home, startled by the sounds of the older woman slamming the front door and bolting it with her key. The birds flapped their wings, climbing toward the gray sky, their caws dying away as the heavy-set figure below trudged down her front walk. The lumbering of her steps, and the sullen expression on her face, gave her the appearance of a woman significantly older than her 63 years.

A blanket of snow had fallen during the night, and icy, crystalline flakes were still coming down as the woman -- the only figure visible in any direction -- walked the length of the dimly lit street. It was a typically dark February morning in Seattle, but the snowfall and the diffused light gave the streets a curious feeling, as though they existed outside of the normal dawn hours.

She slipped a winter cap over a head of gray hair, pulling it down over her ears as she turned onto East Madison, and continued past the stretch of shops that ran through the center of the Madison Park neighborhood. A stream of cold air was blowing in from Lake Washington, driving the icy particles against her weathered face, and causing her brow, forever pinched in a dubious glower, to droop even further over her darkened eyes. She stared at the sidewalk in front of her as she marched on, only occasionally shooting glances to the left and right, primarily to prepare herself for any unwelcome encounters. Aside from the odd dog-walker, whom she made a *particular* effort to circumnavigate, no one bothered her on the walk of a half-dozen blocks.

Uninterested in seeing or being seen, once she turned

onto Lake Washington Boulevard -- a woodsy street that was especially quiet on this snowy morning -- she failed to notice the black sedan that had been following her for several blocks. With her heavy cap and her focus on solitude, she had no clue the vehicle was even there. She also failed to notice when it picked up speed as it rounded the corner after her. The car had closed the gap to less than a block when the driver abruptly swerved to the right, rolled down the window, and extended a gun in a gloved hand. Two shots rang out as bullets struck the woman in the side and the back of the head. The gunshots, and the resulting echoes, rumbled in the winter air, sounding more like the cracks of snow-weary branches than shots from a handgun.

Before the woman's body had even settled in the roadway, the driver's side door opened, and a figure in a dark, shapeless trench coat stepped out, retrieved two shell casings from the snowy ground, returned to the driver's seat, and shifted into reverse. The car struggled to gain traction before it finally caught hold and backed up in a wide arc. The driver shifted back into drive and there was once more a moment of hesitation before the tires dug in and the vehicle took off, slipping and sliding on the slick surface. The driver overcompensated with the accelerator, which caused the car to fishtail half out of control, roaring back and forth across the roadway and briefly running up onto the curb and across a stretch of snow-covered lawn, before ultimately regaining control and racing away.

The sprawled figure lay motionless on the ground some 20 yards away. Snow was quickly gathering on the woman's clothing and drifting around the outline of her lifeless body. The sound of the fleeing vehicle disappeared in the distance as a growing puddle of dark red blood pooled in the once-white snow around the dead woman's head.

A single crow swooped in, landing on a branch overhead, where it surveyed the scene from a distance. Everything was still under the cascading flakes. The crow took a final look at the body below, flapped its wings, and flew away.

I

Brick Ransom blended four cups of flour into the mix of tepid water, salt, and yeast that he'd already stirred together in the non-stick pot. He slipped on the lid to let the mixture rise, and wearily rubbed his square jawline as he gathered his thoughts.

Maybe bread wasn't the smartest thing to be making right now.

While his features remained impressively chiseled and sharp, especially when he considered the declining physical condition of many of his fellow 32-year-olds, Ransom had to admit he was starting to feel his age lately. While he carefully maintained the outward appearance of the former high school football player that he was -- with a trim, yet surprisingly solid build that ably carried a healthy layer of muscle and heft -- the former "Brick" of his high school glory days was definitely feeling the negative effects of his increasing seniority within the Seattle Police Department. And as his level of physical activity declined with each promotion, Ransom was detecting an increasing pinch around his midsection where his pants were growing a little too snug for comfort. For someone who was used to eating whatever and whenever he wanted, it was a jolt to realize he'd have to put in a little effort if he hoped to stay in shape while continuing to hone his culinary skills. And while Brick liked to think that most of the ladies who saw him sans work clothes were caught up in such a tizzy of desire that they wouldn't notice any thickening around his midsection, he was finding it increasingly difficult to kid himself; even if he'd *had* some repeat customers – and frankly, it had been a while – they would likely have noticed that over the last few months he'd begun to wage his own little battle of the bulge. When Brick cross-referenced this realization with the subtle bags under his eyes, and the flecks of silver that were appearing around the temples of his close-cropped hair, homemade bread seemed like a recipe for jowly decline. But it was so damn tasty.

He'd better look into a gym membership that weekend.

There were other matters on his mind today, but the common element through all of them was a general sense of weariness. He poured himself a cup of coffee, picked up a copy of Jean-Claude Renoir's *Gourmet Celebrations,* and headed into the living room, where he slumped into the nearest chair and took a sip of his hot drink.

The coffee, like his mood, was bitter.

He should never have gone cheap on the beans, but he'd blown his grocery budget buying ingredients for the previous night's meal, and as far as breakfast items were concerned, he had, quite uncharacteristically, deemed coffee the lowest item on his list of priorities. He did, however, have a disgusting number of cinnamon sticky buns on hand, for which he'd been honing a variety of double entendres to be delivered while pouring celebratory Mimosas. Unfortunately, the Mimosa components remained bottled, and he hadn't laid a finger on the buns, for the evening before had been an anticlimactic nonstarter. And while he was always one to assign blame to someone else -- preferably Seattle Mayor Nicholas McGuiness whenever possible -- he knew full well that the fiasco of the previous night was entirely a product of his own doing.

His onion tartlet had *not* been a success.

In all the years he'd been whipping up that little seal-the-deal number, Brick had never once suffered such a blistering romantic defeat, but looking back on it, the warning signs had been there from the get-go.

Kelli was a nice enough girl, with a fairly pleasant disposition. Unfortunately, her sense of humor was set far from "ribald sophisticate" and closer to "witless literalist." It was depressing to consider, but Brick had been telling himself for a while now that it was time he recalibrated his rating system. He was 32-years-old, and while he was doing quite well professionally -- the result of joining the police force a few years earlier, just in time to unearth a systemic network of police corruption, which had cleared the path for his very recent promotion to detective -- in his personal life Ransom knew full well it was time he discarded some of his *Seinfeld*-caliber relationship disqualifiers and began to look at the big picture. If a woman was intelligent, sophisticated, attractive, good-hearted, and funny, well, *hell*, that was the ideal combination, but if she was all those things, but didn't meet one or two of his arbitrary qualifiers, maybe, just maybe, he should try to look past that while he explored other areas of their compatibility.

'Course, the importance of some of those categories was weighted more heavily than others.

On their first date, Kelli -- alas, he'd always loved that name -- had asked the waiter at *Ray's* if they had any "bacon mac and cheese," a question which caused Brick to choke on his wine and briefly excuse himself from the table. Upon his return, he'd tried to turn the conversation to recreational pastimes. When she mentioned baseball, he began to feel his mind wandering. As far as Brick knew, baseball involved a stick, a ball, and a few bases. Oh, and it had made for a few pretty good movies. But as far as a regular pastime was concerned, he could never summon enough interest to ponder it any longer than the time it took to drink a beer at the counter of a sports bar. When the dessert menus came, Kelli ignored the crème caramel, *sneered* at the profiteroles, and asked if they had any vanilla ice cream.

Vanilla dinner dates were one thing, but vanilla ice cream was something else entirely!

Normally there would never have been a second date, but at that point Brick was still trying to break his pattern of dysfunction. All he could remember about rendezvous number two was that the bar Kelli had picked had used some sort of pre-packaged margarita mix in their cocktails. The date had gone downhill from there.

Yet foolishly, Brick had still held high hopes for their third go-around when he offered to cook for her at his apartment. He figured the playing field at his place was tilted just enough in his favor to get a fresh start. He could whip up his can't-fail onion tartlet, bowl Kelli over with his culinary skills, work his way past her humorless defenses, and round the bases to home.

Maybe he knew more about baseball than he realized!

Kelli's initial reaction upon seeing his tart involved a Martha Stewart cooking joke that would have been stale back in 1996, but again, Ransom had willed himself to look past it, determined as he was to avoid ending up single and alone till his dying day.

And so, the previous night's revelries had begun at 6:30, when Kelli entered Ransom's cozy one-bedroom apartment, quickly rejected his offer of cabernet after realizing that it was "one of the red ones," declared the tartlet "a little bland," and wondered aloud if some grated cheddar and Tabasco might help it taste "more like Papa Johns." By the time she'd mentioned going home to watch a landscaping program on her DVR, Brick had just wanted her to leave.

As far as dry spells were concerned, this one was starting to seem freeze-dried. Perhaps he could at least start evening up the odds by honing a few of his hero Jean-Claude's more elaborate dishes for the next time he brought a girl back to his place for a meal.

Brick picked up *Gourmet Celebrations*. As far as he was concerned, Jean-Claude Renoir (whose brother Michel – a pharmaceutical researcher - apparently lived in Seattle) was the best of the all time best, a globally renowned chef who Brick had been following on the path to culinary mastery since as far back as he could remember. If Jean-Claude said a recipe or technique worked, Brick took it as gospel. As far as he was concerned, there were two ways to cook: Jean-Claude's way and the wrong way.

The onion tartlet was of course a Renoir masterpiece, but there was always a possibility that Brick had been using the same dish as a gourmet aphrodisiac for a tad too long. Even Musk oil eventually loses it kick.

He flipped through the book as he weighed his options. He needed something rich and elegant, but simple enough that he could whip it up after a long shift out on the streets. It also needed to be light enough that any lass who savored what he'd prepared would still have the energy and gastrointestinal wherewithal to follow the night where it might lead.

He was beginning to narrow down the possibilities. He had the dessert squared away in his mind; he wanted something classic and satisfying, yet playful, fun, and only superficially elegant. For that, he had settled on baked Alaska.

The main course was much trickier. He'd settled on two contenders, but he wasn't sure if either one of them would meet his purposes as nimbly as the onion tartlet had managed to do for all these years. In one corner were lamb loins in ambush with fava beans neyron and leek and mushroom pie. In the other corner was Chateaubriands with Madeira-truffle sauce, mushroom timbales, and crepe shells with corn purée.

Brick took a sip of bitter coffee, grimaced, and rubbed his chin in thought. He supposed it all depended on-

His cell phone vibrated as Bob Seger's "Shakedown" started to play.

Damn. He should have turned the ringer off.

A few years ago he wouldn't have been caught dead with one of these damn things, now he couldn't seem to function without it. Being easily reachable had its drawbacks. He'd been hoping his first couple of weeks in investigations would be slow, let him coast a little bit, maybe "work from home" as he hammered the kinks out of the new recipes. With any luck this was just an administrative call and not someone telling him there had been a murder. Brick stood and walked into the kitchen as he pulled the phone from his pocket.

"Brick Ransom here."

His new partner, David O'Brien, was on the other end of the line.

"Okay, Lake Washington Boulevard," Brick said as he eyed the pink bakery box full of cinnamon buns. "I'll be there in 30 minutes."

Brick slipped the pot of bread dough into the fridge to let it rise. Then he downed the rest of his coffee, grabbed a sticky bun for the road, and headed for the front hall. He stopped halfway there, returned to the kitchen for the rest of the buns, and took the box with him as he headed out the door.

*   *   *

Traffic was moving quicker than he'd expected given the fresh snowfall, and even with a few slips and slides in his old cruiser, Brick arrived at his destination just about on time. If he'd had the patience to put on his snow chains, he might even have gotten there earlier than predicted. Either way, in spite of the driving conditions, he'd managed to eat another one of those damn cinnamon buns on the way. He could already feel the growing bubble of self-loathing swelling in his belly; it seemed to have settled in his lower gut, as his pants were feeling even *snugger* around his waistline. He'd be happy to unload some of these pastries. He should never have bought the damn things in the first place.

He took in the scene as he rounded the corner and emerged on an open stretch of roadway, where police cars, an ambulance, and a swarm of uniformed officers had commandeered the area. No matter how many times he saw it, Ransom never tired of the sight of patrol cars parked around the perimeter of an early morning crime scene -- their sirens off, their lights revolving silently across the darkened landscape of the locale du jour; it invariably sent a shiver of adrenaline up his spine. On the rare occasions the press was on the scene when he got there, Brick had come dangerously close to giggling out loud from the excitement of it all. 'Course, now that he was on homicide, the excitement was coupled with more than a tinge of dread. Someone was dead; otherwise none of these people would be here.

His status as a homicide detective was still settling in. It had been under a month, and truth be told, he wasn't sure he was entirely suited to the job. He'd always thought of himself as less of a details guy, and more of the rampaging bull sort. His headstrong, half-assed style had served him well over the last few years, but he wasn't sure how his methods would translate to investigation.

Brick found a parking spot along the side of the road and briefly wished he had one of those red lights to stick on the roof of his unmarked vehicle. He kept meaning to ask the guys at the maintenance garage how he might go about getting one of them, but so far he'd-

Bam! Bam! Bam!

Brick damn near jumped out of his skin at the sound of someone knocking on his window. He turned and saw David O'Brien, a handsome African American man six years his senior, looking in the driver's side window at him. He'd been casually teamed with O'Brien since moving into investigations, and though he sensed his more senior "partner" -- for lack of a better term -- wasn't quite sure what to make of his younger, greener counterpart, Ransom had never detected any feelings of resentment or mistrust. If anything, O'Brien couldn't have been any more welcoming. After the shakeups that had rattled the department over the last few years, due largely to events in which Brick had played a central role, he got the feeling O'Brien respected him, but had chosen to keep some protective barriers up. Plus, Brick was well aware of the fact that unlike himself, David was married, and he and his wife had their hands quite full with twin two-year-old girls at home. As always, O'Brien was clad in a flawlessly pressed suit under a tan trench coat. Brick on the other hand was dressed in jeans, an untucked button-down shirt, and lace-up Keen sneakers. Today, owing to the temperature, he was also wearing a heavy winter coat.

Brick cracked the door as he reached for the cinnamon buns.

O'Brien was always helpful when it came to unloading junk food.

"Ransom," O'Brien said. "About time you got here."

"What are you talking about?" Brick asked as he held the pastries out as a peace offering. "I headed over the minute you called me!"

"Funny how *I'm* always the first to get called down to these things. A person might almost suspect you'd paid dispatch to bump me to the top of the notification list."

"Now, why would I do that?" Brick asked innocently.

He had in fact done exactly that.

"Stop the conspiracy talk and have a cinnamon roll."

O'Brien eyed the pink box suspiciously. "I really don't need to be eating that stuff…"

"But?" Brick coaxed…

"But just one won't hurt." O'Brien reasoned as he quickly extracted a bun and took a bite. "You're a dietary saboteur, you know that?"

Brick ignored the accusation as he gathered his things together and climbed out of the car, bringing the pink bakery box with him.

"Now," he continued as they headed toward the nexus of police officers. "What are we looking at?"

"White female. 63-years-old. Shot twice from a bit of a distance -- once in the side, once in the back of the head."

"Any witnesses?"

"None that we know of. Body was covered with a couple

inches of snow by the time a woman walked by with her dog and called it in."

"And where is she?" Brick asked.

O'Brien motioned to a blond-haired patrol officer, who was standing near the corner of Lake Washington and East Madison, directing traffic away from the scene. "Vanderburg over there took her statement as soon as he got here. Sent her on her way afterward. That was about an hour ago."

Brick nodded as they approached the center of activity. He held the box of pastries out in front of him.

"Cinnamon roll?" Ransom asked as a uniformed officer walked past.

The young man smiled and motioned to his stomach. Cops were always on guard against outgrowing their bulletproof jackets. Hours spent in patrol cars grew *especially* uncomfortable if your belly fat started getting pinched between your body armor and the top of your belt.

"So, she was in the roadway here for what, about an hour, before someone found her?" Brick theorized.

"That's what we think. Snow was coming down pretty steady for a while. Like I said, a fair amount of it had settled on the body by the time we got here."

Several officers were gathered around cars that were blocking the crime scene from view of the road. They nodded at Ransom and O'Brien as they approached. Brick again held out the pink box.

O'Brien watched several more officers beg off the pastries before he finally chimed in. "Dammit people! Eat some of those things before I end up downing the entire box myself!"

A few of the younger guys exchanged looks, grabbed some pastries, and went back to their discussions.

By the time Ransom and O'Brien approached a woman in her mid-40s, Brick was down to just two rolls. She was dressed in form-fitting winter weather gear with a wool cap pulled down over medium-length silver hair, and had been filling out paperwork while occasionally looking at the ground, where a sheet of thick white plastic was pulled over the unmistakable shape of a body. A ring of brownish-red slush was visible along the edges of the sheet, but it was mostly buried under the snow that had fallen since the time of the shooting.

The woman smiled when she glanced up and saw Brick approaching.

"Sweet buns?" Brick asked, his tone suggesting he'd overlooked the question mark.

"You better watch yourself, man," O'Brien interjected. "You're gonna get caught up in a harassment investigation."

"What?" Brick exclaimed innocently. "I'm just spreading some comfort, helping people cope.

"*Sure* you are, Ransom." The woman replied with a smile.

Anne Sullivan was the SPD's jack of all trades wherever forensics were concerned. She analyzed crime scenes, took photos, and offered her two cents whenever it was called for. She was also one of Brick's favorite people in the department, mostly because she gave as good as she got. Anne was funny, good-natured, beautiful, and, unfortunately for Ransom, very happily married.

"Would you please take one of those things," David said as he held up his own half-eaten bun.

"Of course," Anne replied as she reached into the box.

"My wife thanks you," O'Brien replied as he finished his own roll and tucked his shirt in around his stomach.

"What can you tell us so far, Anne?" Brick asked.

"Are you going to make me do the usual lift-the-sheet-and-share-my hypothesis routine again?"

"I'm afraid I don't know any other way."

Anne walked over to the sheet, switched the pastry to her other hand, crouched down, and lifted the plastic, offering Brick a good look at the body as she took a bite of her cinnamon roll.

Brick always winced at the first glimpse of a body, but once his eyes knew what areas to avoid lingering over, a look at the victim was often extremely helpful. From the way the remains of this victim's nose and face were smashed in, Ransom guessed she had fallen to the ground face first.

"Who turned her over?"

"That would be me," Anne answered.

Brick looked up and down the street, then motioned towards East Madison. "And you think the shots came from that direction?"

"We're sure of it," O'Brien said. "We've got tire tracks, a spot where someone got out of a car for a moment, and that's it. Only other vehicles that have been through here since this morning were police and EMT. The tracks have filled in with snow, but it looks like the shooter's car pulled up behind her there, fired off two rounds, then turned around and drove off like a bat out of hell. Whoever did it must have been a pretty cool customer; we couldn't find any shell casings, so we think they had the presence of mind to stop and clean up after themselves."

Anne interjected, "Well, they might have been cool at the start, but I'm guessing adrenaline got the better of them as they took off, 'cause it looks like they lost control and ran up on the sidewalk on the west side of the street there for a little ways before they straightened out the vehicle and took off."

Brick's eyes traveled from one point to the next as he gauged the distance from the body to the spot where the car had been stopped, and again to the area where it had apparently run up on the side. He focused his attention back on the body.

"Do we know who she is?" he asked.

"Yeah, *D. J. Norman*," O'Brien said, emphasizing the name in a way that made Brick look up.

"You make it sound like I should know her."

O'Brien and Anne exchanged glances.

"D. J. Norman?" Anne repeated.

"D.J., like a *deejay* DJ?"

"I told you," O'Brien said to Anne. "Unless she'd written a cookbook, Brick wouldn't know her."

The tone left Brick feeling a little peeved. "So, she's a writer?"

"Yeah," Anne replied. "D. J. stands for Diane Joan Norman, she's a fairly well-known Seattle mystery writer."

"Why the 'DJ' part?"

"Her publisher initially had her publish under her initials so readers wouldn't know she was a woman. Thought they'd sell more books that way," O'Brien said.

"Seems a little sexist, doesn't it?" Brick asked.

"She's been writing for a *long* time," Anne said. "I used to read her stuff when I was in college."

"Interesting," Brick said as he walked away.

He stopped at the spot where the shooter's car had pulled over. O'Brien followed close behind. Brick looked around for a moment, then continued on to the area where the driver

Michael Attebery

had bounced over the curb and torn up the ground between the road and a concrete walkway. He held his chin in thought for a moment and turned around in a half-circle to look back over the roadway.

A sports field sat off to his left, tucked away from traffic. Trees grew in dense formations on either side of the street, their leafless winter branches stretched out overhead. There were a few houses off to the right some distance from the road, and a few more homes were just barely visible on the far end of the field on the left.

"Schools closed for the day?" he asked finally.

"Yeah, I think so," O'Brien said. "Why?"

"Kids tend to get up early on snow days. Lets have a couple of guys canvas the area today, see if they can find any kids who were out playing and might have seen something."

O'Brien nodded.

"Do we know where she lived?" Brick asked.

"We do. Not too far from here actually. I was over there earlier. We've still got a team locking things down."

~

Brick followed O'Brien's car down Madison and into a residential neighborhood a few blocks to the west. They pulled up in front of a modest looking house with two squad cars parked in the driveway. It seemed this case was warranting a heavier response than usual. Knowing a bit more about the victim now, it was starting to make sense.

Brick parked his car and walked up the driveway. It was a low-key home, a brick one-story, probably from the 50s, nice but certainly not ostentatious. It had probably been one of the more expensive places in the area when it went up, but now it was simply a classic, above-market home for the modestly well to do. The property seemed to be meticulously cared for: the trees and plants cut back from the house, the shutters and trim well maintained, no peeling paint in sight. It didn't look like D. J. Norman had been much for gardening or lawn ornaments. Aside from a sign reading "No Dogs," the yard was practically bare.

O'Brien led the way into the house. The place smelled like mothballs, and while the interior, like the front yard, appeared to be impeccably clean, an odd atmosphere hung in the air, like the home hadn't been entirely *lived* in for years. Everything was just a little too squared off, a little too exact, like the owner had declared her dominion over these few rooms, and made the decision to keep all outsiders at bay. Then again, maybe it was just the orange couch and the avocado carpet that seemed out of sync with the outside world. The décor was undeniably dated, even as it was slavishly maintained *just so*. Brick followed O'Brien through the living room and into the open kitchen and dining area, both of which had the same dreary green and orange palate.

"I feel like a wormhole just pulled me back to my childhood," Brick muttered.

O'Brien nodded. "I know what you mean. This place is like my grandmother's house. Vintage, but not the kind that sells."

Two uniformed officers were working their way through the rest of the home. Ransom could see them occasionally cross the hallway in the background as they swept the remaining rooms. He looked at O'Brien expectantly.

"There was no sign of a struggle," O'Brien began. "No signs of forced entry. Nothing appears to have been disturbed. A plate with some toast crumbs in the sink. A half-read paper on the kitchen table. Looks like she got up, got dressed, followed her typical morning routine, then went out for a walk and was shot dead."

Brick noticed two black Moleskine notebooks on the table beside the folded newspaper. An empty coffee cup sat beside them.

"Is she married? Any kids?"

"Never married. No kids, either."

"Any relatives? Anybody close to her in town?" Bricked continued, thinking aloud as he looked around the room.

"We're looking into it," O'Brien said, "but it's doubtful. She had a bit of an… antisocial reputation. From everything we've been able to tell, she wrote her books and kept to herself."

"Hmm. Anyone looked at those journals?"

"Not yet."

Brick approached the table, taking a closer look at the notebooks. The corner of a business card was sticking out from under one of them. He reached into his pocket and withdrew a pen, which he pressed down on the card and used to slide it out from under the Moleskine.

The card read:

Karl Ryan – Owner
Cryptic Bindings - Mystery Bookshop
212 First Avenue *South*
Seattle, WA 98104

Ransom searched around for a scrap of paper, then he jotted down the information and slipped it into his pocket.

"Can you do me a favor?" He asked as he headed for the

door. "After Anne and the boys do whatever they need to do around here, could you take a look at these notebooks and see if you can find anything useful in them?"

O'Brien nodded. "Will do."

"Also, I know this is pretty standard-issue stuff, but see what you can find out about her. Does anyone benefit from this lady being out of the picture?"

"No problem. Where are you headed?"

"I'm gonna do a little book shopping," Brick replied.

*   *   *

The bookshop's ancient brass bell, caked with years of dust and downtown grime, barely chimed as Brick pushed the door shut behind him and looked around. Row after row of neatly aligned books, their spines and covers all facing the ceiling, lay stretched out on the tables before him. A staircase on the left side of the room climbed up to a loft area, where still more books peered down from the shelves overhead. A man in his 50s, with thinning hair and small round glasses, sat in the back of the room, reading a newspaper.

Ransom wandered the tables for a minute, trying his best to get the lay of the place. It seemed classic and contemporary mysteries were intermixed, with no single table containing only new releases or current bestsellers. Everything was clearly organized in *some* sort of order, but for someone who usually focused on cookbooks and biographies, Brick was struggling to get his bearings. Finally, unable to crack the store's system of organization, he headed to the back to get some assistance.

The man with the paper looked up instinctively as he heard the footsteps starting in his direction.

"Can I help you with something?" he asked as Brick

stepped closer.

The man spoke with a strong Irish accent, which Brick felt was somehow perfect for a quiet shop filled with mysteries.

"I'm hoping you can," Brick replied. "You wouldn't happen to be Karl Ryan, would you?"

The man's eyebrows rose slightly.

"Yes, I am."

"Brick Ransom, I'm with the Seattle police," Brick said as he presented his badge. "I have a few questions for you."

Ryan glanced at the shield nervously, clearly taken aback by the gesture, "What can I do for you?"

"Well, for starters, I was wondering if you could tell me how you know D. J. Norman."

Ryan blinked as he processed the question, then he shook his head slightly. "I really *don't* know her, but as a matter of fact, I just met her last weekend at a mystery expo where I was selling books by the event speakers. I struck up a conversation with her when she came to my booth to see how her titles were selling."

"So she was one of the speakers?" Brick asked.

"Yes."

"And how *were* her books selling?"

Ryan pointed to a stack of open boxes near the bottom of the stairs. "See for yourself. Not all that great, unfortunately."

Brick crossed the room to take a closer look. The boxes contained a large number of mass-market paperbacks and around a half-dozen hardcover editions. "These are all hers?"

Ryan nodded as he walked over. "Yep. The hardcover titles are her first book, *Sub Rosa*. That one always sells well. The paperbacks are her latest release, *Dead Men Don't*."

"Don't *what?*"

"Don't sell any books apparently."

"Not a big seller, huh?"

"That would be putting it mildly. It's another turkey of a release. She's had a string of them the last few years. I'm sending most of them back to the publisher for credit."

"Why don't the new ones sell?" Brick asked as he ran his fingers over the spines of *Dead Men Don't*.

"You want *my* opinion?" Ryan mused as he drew one hand to his chin. "There's just something missing since she jumped ship and went with one of the big publishers back East." He picked up the nearest paperback copy of *Dead Men Don't,* tore off the front, and handed Ransom the coverless book. "You can see for yourself if you like." On seeing Ransom's surprised expression, he elaborated, "Oh, for mass-market returns the publisher just takes the front cover and credits my account. The cost of shipping paperbacks *back* is more than what the books are even worth." He pointed to the barcode on the inside of the torn cover. "They scan this thing here, then we're supposed to toss the books. I sort of hate for them to go to waste though, so I usually drop them off at shelters or stack them by the back dumpster for someone to snag. Why are you wondering about Norman, anyways?"

"Well, I'm sorry to say it, but she's dead."

Ryan took a step back. "You're kidding me. What happened?"

"She was murdered."

"That's *terrible.* When did this happen?"

"Sometime early this morning." Brick watched Ryan closely. "The reason I'm here is that your business card was sitting on her kitchen table when we searched her house. I was hoping you might be able to help us fill in a few gaps as we start our investigation."

Ryan leaned against the nearest table, looking increasingly disoriented. "What a strange thing. Like I said, I didn't even know her, I just met her at that event and had talked to her about coming in this week and signing some books for the shop."

"But not these books here?"

Ryan hesitated before he answered. "Well, no. I had her sign a few paperback copies of her newer books at the event, but even those didn't sell terribly well. I was mostly hoping to have her sign some hardcover copies of her first book when I got more in. The older books, especially *Sub Rosa,* are the ones that people want. I only asked her to sign a few of the newer ones to stay on her good side."

"Good side?"

"You really don't know much about Diane Norman yet, do you? They say to speak no ill of the dead, but let me put it this way, the common opinion in the book community was that she was a temperamental, vindictive piece of work. I got a glimpse of that firsthand last weekend."

"So, you had a run in with her?"

"Thankfully, no, but like I said, I had a booth at that event, and I was sitting at my table in the back of the auditorium when she did a joint Q & A with Daniel Buckley – he's her former publisher's current top-seller. Apparently Norman still has some bad blood with the imprint-"

"And who was her former publisher?" Brick interrupted.

"She used to be with Catacomb Press. They're a Seattle mystery publisher specializing in pulpy, hard-boiled detective stuff. The kind of books I focus on, actually."

Brick jotted the name down. "Catacomb. Could you give me a little background on them?"

"Sure. Norman started out with Catacomb about 20 years ago, when both she and the Press' owner, Maureen Alexander, were just getting started in the business. The marketing story was that Norman was a real estate agent back then and wrote her books in the mornings before work. Alexander was just out of college and green enough to take a shot at publishing. They struck gold together when Maureen started Catacomb and put *Sub Rosa* out as their first book."

"And from what you said, I gather Norman is no longer working with this Maureen-?"

"Alexander," Ryan finished. "No. Norman was Catacomb's bread and butter headliner up until about five years ago when her books start getting panned, and Maureen started publishing some titles from a new guy, Daniel Buckley. Pretty quick Buckley's sales were leaving Norman's stuff in the dust. Word around here was that she'd lost her touch, and she resented a new guy coming in who was still on his game."

"So she bailed," Brick guessed.

"Yes she did, she left and got a bigger contract with one of the mega-conglomerate publishers, but unfortunately, she brought her losing streak with her. Meanwhile, the up-and-coming name on the pulp mystery scene became Dan Buckley."

"And Buckley was the person she was appearing with at the Q and A? I wonder who cooked *that* idea up. Did she get into an argument with him?"

"Buckley? No, not directly, but she really ripped into him. Every time someone asked her a question, she somehow found a way to twist it around and turn it into a scathing assessment of Buckley's stuff, especially his latest book, *Cheap Thrills*."

Brick nodded, "I've heard about that one, actually"

"Probably because it's been making the New York Times Bestseller list its bitch-" Ryan caught himself and laughed. "It's been doing very well, which was getting under Norman's skin I think. Like I said, every one of her comments about the current state of mystery writing had a little dig about Buckley's stuff and the "cheap thrills" readers were apparently looking for these days. He handled it like a total gentleman though. He's a class act. Younger, but he has something, a sort of polish that will only help him over time I think."

"So, you know him…"

"Not well, but he's been in the shop a few times. He's an excellent writer and really generous with his readers."

Brick looked around. "Do you have any of his books here?"

"Sorry, I'm sold out."

"Of course. So, if Norman didn't get into it with Buckley, and she was decent enough to you, what happened at that event?"

"After the talk, and after she came over to chat with me, I was in front of the convention center loading the unsold books into my van, when I saw Norman approach Maureen Alexander and completely tear into her. It sounded like real old, real bad blood. She was complaining about royalties on her old titles, saying something about Alexander's 'boy-toy Dan Buckley' not having to grovel to get his royalty checks on time, just a ton of what sounded like ancient, bitter history between them."

"And how did Ms. Alexander handle it?"

"Maureen gave as good as she got, defended herself against every one of the charges, and got in a few digs about Norman chasing after the big checks, ditching Catacomb, and losing her edge."

'Doesn't sound like Alexander's any pushover herself.' Brick observed.

"Maureen can be a charmer, and she's a hell of a force in local publishing, but yeah, she's cutthroat."

"You wouldn't happen to have a way I could get ahold of her, would you?"

"Actually, yes. I can give you her number." Ryan headed over to his desk at the back and grabbed a piece of paper. He held it up so Brick could see the front of it, which read *'Slash and Grab: The Case of the Modern Detective Story.'* "I'll give you a copy of the flyer from the event. Maybe it will be helpful," he said as he jotted a number down on the back of the pamphlet.

"That would be great. Thanks for the paperback too." Brick said as he pulled out his wallet. "While you're at it, could I pick up a copy of *Sub Rosa*, just for comparison?"

"Absolutely," Ryan replied as he handed Brick the flyer and grabbed a copy of the late D.J. Norman's bestselling title, which he wrapped in brown paper and tied with a ribbon. He nodded at the torn, coverless paperback Brick was holding, then handed him the neatly wrapped hardcover, giving the top a gentle tap as he let go. "This is how I *prefer* to sell books here. I hope I've been of some help."

"No question," Brick replied as he handed Ryan his VISA card and one of his SPD business cards. "If you hear of anything else, please give me a ring."

*　　*　　*

Steelhead Diner was Brick's idea of the perfect Seattle restaurant. Casual and airy, not too loud, but with impeccable service that rivaled the most formal dining establishments in town. Plus, they served the best damn tater tots Brick had ever tasted. Fried to a heavenly gold, containing just the right amount of Dungeness crab meat, they had a deliciously rich, yet remarkably airy quality that had left him feeling dangerously full on more than one occasion. Yet they went down so easily, and were so utterly delicious, that he could eat a few dozen of them without taking a breath. As it was, he ordered two happy hour servings, half of which he washed down with a White Russian as he waited for Flynn to arrive. He'd already taken the liberty of opening the tab under his friend's name.

Brick sat at the bar and looked out the window. From here he had a perfect angle of the beer handles, the specials menu, and a sunset view of The Market, with Puget Sound and Bainbridge Island in the background. A ferry was cutting across the water in the fading pink glow, its lights rippling over the surface as it glided behind the famed Pike Place sign. This was always his favorite time of day, when work and the pressure of feeling that he should be *accomplishing* something gave way to the routines of happy hour and the synchronized machinations of the city's food enthusiasts. He'd likely ponder the case a bit more when he got home, the work was always doing backflips in the back of his mind no matter what he was doing, but for now, it was time to relax and unwind.

He recognized many of the diners scattered around the room. They, like himself, were members of a virtual army of eager restaurant goers who fanned out across the city most weeknights, moving in criss-crossing patterns of foodie fanaticism as they sampled new restaurants and returned again and again to old favorites. Steelhead was a typical Tuesday night stop, one he often made with his friend, and one which they frequently took the liberty of charging to Flynn's dining account with *The Seattle Post-Intelligencer.* So far they had been lucky, no one at the paper had questioned their resident critic's reason for "reviewing" the established winner on an almost weekly basis. Sooner or later Brick knew they have to start springing for the check themselves, but until Flynn's editor noticed the pattern and put an end to it, they'd continue helping themselves to some of the best food and drink in town.

Brick noticed his glass was empty, and had just motioned to the waitress to grab her attention, when he turned and saw his old friend walking in the door. Flynn Davis, like Brick, was 32 years old and an almost lifelong Seattleite. Aside from the four years he'd spent back East for college, he'd always lived in the area. After graduation, through fate or simple happenstance, he and his college sweetheart Morgan had both found jobs in the Emerald City, and the two of them had been in town and together ever since. Unlike Ransom, who retained a hint of his former football player build, but was struggling to ward off a touch of unwelcome thickness recently, Flynn was as rail thin as he had been in high school, with an almost Obama-like frame. This was all the more remarkable given his occupation – the man was literally *paid* to sit and eat and sit and write about what he had eaten while sitting! He had a boyish quality that had never left him. Smooth, narrow face. Short hair. A lightness in his step that most guys seemed to lose around the time they took their first desk job. The only signs that he was over 30 were the whisps of gray around his temples, and the faintest of lines under her eyes (and those had only appeared in the last couple of years).

The bartender came over and Brick took the liberty of ordering Manhattans for both of them.

Manhattans were Flynn Davis' longtime weakness. His only weakness, so far as Brick could tell. For a guy who had worked at the same paper since college -- starting on the sports page, moving to obits and the police blotter, and finally settling into the food critic gig he'd always wanted -- the fact that his biggest vice in daily life was one of the classics of classic cocktails, told you quite a bit about the man. Manhattans, so far as Brick was concerned, were an older man's drink. He loved them, but he could never have one without picturing himself seated in a perfectly worn leather chair, in a paneled den, watching classic episodes of *Magnum P.I.* The fact that each sip summoned a day in the life image from the life of an older man only reinforced his prototypical characterization of the drink.

Flynn crossed the room, slapping Ransom on the shoulder as he sat down.

"How are you?"

"Not too bad," Brick said a half second before the bartender returned with their drinks.

"You took the liberty of ordering for me I see."

"The least I can do considering you're paying for it."

Flynn gave him a look. "We've really got to stop doing that. I keep waiting to find a disciplinary notice in my mailbox."

"Please, they owe you," Brick said.

"I'd like to think that, but you know as well as I do how good that place has been to me over the years. They've paid for my house, my car, and I don't know how many lab tests and ultrasounds-"

Brick looked at him. "How's that going?"

Flynn took a sip of his drink and knocked on the bar.

"So far so good. Morgan has a good feeling this time."

"Good."

The noise in the restaurant had picked up a little, but the plate of tater tots still made an audible scraping sound as Flynn slid it closer and popped one of them into his mouth.

"So," he asked. "How are things with *you?*"

"Well, they haven't been as laid back as I was hoping they'd be at this point. As of today I've got one murder on my hands."

"You mean *case.*"

"What?"

"You've got one murder *case* on your hands. I hope that's what you mean at least. You're supposed be *solving* crimes, not committing them."

"Oh. Yeah. Case," Brick replied.

"I was actually wondering how things were going with you personally," Flynn said. "But we can talk shop if you like."

"Well, now that you mention it, maybe you'll know something I don't. You have any information on D.J. Norman?"

"I do actually, but isn't she a little old for you?"

"The hell are you talking about? I thought we were discussing work."

"We are, I'm just joking. Yeah, I know a bit about Diane

Norman. I crossed paths with her once or twice a few years ago when I was still covering the police blotter and she was researching the Seattle Police Department for one of her mysteries. She been bothering you, too?"

"Well, no, not her personally. She's dead."

Flynn turned to him. "Dead? *Really?*"

"Shot in the back this morning."

Flynn fished the cherry from the bottom of his Manhattan. "I hate to say this, but that doesn't surprise me at all. That lady was a real piece of work."

"So people keep telling me. How so?"

"Oh, off the top of my head. She was mean, arrogant, cruel, condescending, abusive, pedantic-"

"We could just as easily be discussing my last date."

"Kelli?" Flynn asked.

Brick shrugged. "I'm kidding, too. She was nice enough, just a bore."

"Are we talking about Kelli or Diane Norman?"

"All right, cut it out." Brick got serious. "First, Diane Norman is dead. Do you know anything that could explain who might have wanted to bump her off?"

"Might be easier to write up a list of the folks who *didn't* want to bump her off." Flynn thought for a moment. "Lots of folks I can imagine would have wanted that old broad dead. She was a nasty customer. But, who specifically? That I don't know. I'll think about it though, tell you if anything comes to mind."

"I'd appreciate it."

"Now, can we talk about the big date? What went haywire with Kelli?"

"What didn't" Brick replied.

"Over and done with then?"

"Without question."

"I owe Morgan money. She said you wouldn't make it past three dates. I thought you might be ready to break the pattern."

"Thanks a whole hell of a lot, man!"

Flynn raised his open hand as if to say 'what can I tell ya?'

The ice in Brick's glass made a tinkling sound as Flynn studied his expression. He leaned back in his chair.

"So, now what's the plan?"

"Plan?" Ransom shrugged his shoulders. "Mail order bride?"

"I'm being serious."

"So am I! Well, not "bride" serious, but I was really hoping I could make this one work."

"The champagne problems of the ladies' man," Flynn muttered before he caught Brick's expression and knew the window for jokes had closed. "Look, the whole 'making it work' thing, that just may be your problem. You need to approach the next opportunity with an open mind; see it as one potential route to the next stage in your life. Don't decide the next one will without question be *the one,* but at the same time, don't put up the same defenses you always do. Be open to the universe's possibilities."

"I don't even know what that means. That sounds like a bunch of nonsense."

"OK, yeah, the Manhattan is not my beverage of clarity." Flynn swallowed a large gulp and continued. "Last time we talked I got the sense you were ready to get more serious about dating."

"I am."

"And you were sure you could find the right person on your own."

"I was."

"But, that doesn't appear to be the case."

Brick nodded. "Apparently not."

"So… maybe I can help."

"You're talking about that girl again, the one from work that you've been trying to set me up with."

"I'm telling you, she's perfect! She's funny, she's interesting, and she's *beautiful*!"

"You said the same think about Morgan's friend Vicky about nine years ago."

"Yeah, I know, but in my defense, who other than *you* keeps a bottle of Bacardi 151 around the house after college?"

"She tried to *kill me,* man!"

Flynn shrugged. "These things happen."

Brick shot him a look. "Seriously, have you *ever* known a Vicky who wasn't bad news?"

"No. I suppose I haven't. But in my defense, things were different back then."

"Different how?"

"First of all, that was ten years ago, and I didn't really know her, I was just trying to get on Morgan's good side. I really didn't think that girl was for you, and I certainly didn't expect her to set your apartment on fire."

"Thank you!"

"But I'm telling you, if I wasn't married, I'd ask this girl out myself."

"Here's a question for you. If she's so perfect, why is she single?"

"Well, she wasn't single when she moved out here, but she and her boyfriend split up last year; he went back to Austin, and she says she never meets anyone new 'cause she's always at the movies."

"Doesn't that seem sort of… pathetic?"

"She's the *PI*'s film critic! Remember?"

"All right, fine."

"Fine what?" Flynn was dubious.

"Set it up."

"OK." Flynn reached for a tater tot, and was about to take a bite, but paused. "You're sure?"

Brick nodded.

"Now we're talking," Flynn said with a smile as he popped the tot in his mouth. "Now we're talking."

*   *   *

It was dark by the time Brick pulled onto North 84th and found a parking space on the street. He climbed out of the car with a groan and tucked the books from Cryptic Bindings under his arm.

The Dean was a brick apartment building in Seattle's Greenwood neighborhood. The building had been built in 1927, and more than eight decades later, it still looked much the same as it had when it was completed. Once folks moved into the building, they seemed to stay for as long as they could before jobs or growing families took them elsewhere. Brick had been there for almost ten years – he'd moved there after the infamous "Vicky the Pyromaniac" episode – and he had no plans to go anywhere. The building was warm, well managed, and felt like home.

He let himself into the lobby, where he checked his mail and headed up the creaking stairs as he sorted through

the letters. He was relieved there were no bills, nothing
he'd feel the need to attend to immediately, just a copy of
Architectural Digest, the latest issue of Martha Stewart
Living, two envelopes of coupons and offers for neighborhood
business, and a couple of odd circulars. He had sorted
through everything by the time he reached the third floor
and opened the door to 304.

Brick cut through the darkened front hall and headed
straight for the kitchen, where he set the oven to 425 before
cutting back through, dropping the books and his cell phone
on the dining room table, and depositing the mail on top of
a bookshelf just to the right of the entrance to the walk-in
closet. By the time he'd changed out of his work clothes and
into a pair of sweats and a Nick Tahou's t-shirt, the buzzer
had gone off for the kitchen. He took the pot of dough from
the fridge, removed the top, and slid it into the oven, setting
the timer for one hour. He fixed himself one last White
Russian and settled down in the living room with the two D.
J. Norman books.

He started with *Dead Men Don't,* and struggled through
a grueling five pages before he started to nod off. His chin
had just dropped to his chest when he jolted awake, catching
himself a split second before he would have spilled his drink.

Never let a bad book cost you a cocktail!

He took a sip, tossed the paperback aside, and picked up
Sub Rosa.

The second D.J. Norman book, actually her first, was a
corker. Good characters. Good story. Hell of a pace. He'd
made it through the first fifty pages by the time the buzzer
sounded again. Brick grabbed another sip of his drink and
returned to the kitchen, where he removed the baked bread

from the oven, shook the round loaf free of the pan, and set it on a wire rack to cool.

Ransom headed to the closet, where he searched through his jacket pockets till he found the flyer Karl Ryan had given him that afternoon. He flipped it over and dialed the number the bookseller had scrawled on the back. As he'd expected at this hour, Maureen Alexander's voicemail picked up.

"Good evening, Ms. Alexander. This is Detective Brick Ransom with the Seattle Police Department. It's around 10 p.m. Tuesday night. I'm wondering if you can give me a call at your earliest convenience. My number is (206) 327-7198. Thank you very much."

Brick set the phone down and returned to his chair. The wind was blowing outside, and a gentle but frigid draft of winter air blew past his feet as he sat by the window reading. As if on cue, the radiator by the entrance to the kitchen burbled as the heat came on. Brick flipped the page and pulled the book closer. He couldn't wait to see how this one was going to play out.

*   *   *

Bob Seger jolted him awake at the crack of dawn.

He really needed to find a more soothing ringtone.

Ransom jumped to his feet, lunging for his phone as *Sub Rosa* tumbled from his lap.

"Ransom here," he mumbled into the handset.

"Detective Ransom, This is Maureen Alexander," The woman on the other end announced. Brick glanced at the clock on his cable box: 6:57 a.m. "I hope I didn't wake you," Alexander said chipperly.

"Oh, no, no," Brick began as he rubbed his weary eyes. "I was just-"

Alexander cut him off as she continued talking, and Brick instantly realized that this was someone who said polite things, like *"I hope I didn't wake you,"* but who didn't really care what a person's response might be.

"I'm returning your call," She continued. "Would you happen to have time to come by my office this morning?"

'Certainly," Brick replied.

"Excellent, my assistant will give you directions," Alexander said in conclusion, just before she put him on hold and Brick was left listening to a muzak rendition of *Against the Wind.*

He *really* needed to change his ringtone.

A seaplane swept in overhead as Brick slipped across Dexter Avenue and into South Lake Union. The roads were much easier to maneuver today than they had been the previous morning. That was Seattle for you. One day you might have torrential rain, the next a transient snowstorm, the next, clear skies and sunny streetscapes. At the moment, while the weather wasn't exactly sweltering, the streets were dry as a bone and safer than a Jack Johnson album.

Catacomb Press had just moved into an impressive new building in the up-and-coming neighborhood. Ransom had seen it written up in an issue of *Pacific Northwest Magazine* a few weeks earlier, and he recognized the place the moment he rounded the corner.

As he pulled his beat-up cruiser into a Catacomb-reserved curbside spot in front of the building, Brick spotted a black 2013 BMW parked in front of a sign reading: M. Alexander.

So, the grand poomba was definitely in the office.

Brick's eyes moved from the Catacomb owner's

immaculately maintained vehicle, to the shiny new building. Despite the unseasonably cold temperatures outside, the glass and steel building seemed remarkably warm and welcoming, especially for such a modern design.

He tried to recall everything he could from the magazine's write-up. It had been one of the all too rare architectural pieces written by Valerie Easton, as opposed to the convoluted cutesy stuff the magazine's regular writer churned out most weeks, so Brick had actually been able to read the piece from beginning to end before he began salivating over the photo spread. As Brick entered the building's main foyer -- a surprisingly large, completely open area on the first floor -- the images from the magazine came rushing back to him, filling in the gaps between what his eyes saw, and what he remembered reading about.

The offices, like so many great building these days, had been designed by Tom Kundig and built by Yellow Dog Construction. Though ninety percent of the structure was new, there were a few remnants of the location's original building preserved throughout. While the bulk of the structure consisted primarily of three stories of glass and steel, with weathered, tastefully rusting metal exposed to the elements on the outside, the interior revealed the fact that the building was actually a meticulously crafted three-walled shell, one that used the last of the lot's original brick warehouse walls as its fourth and final piece. The roof was composed of jet-black steel beams that stretched from the brick back wall, across to the front, where they rested on the shoulders of their newer glass and steel mates. The beams were then topped with corrugated metal that had been punched through with skylights every five to ten feet. As with all of Kundig's buildings, there were gadgets, massive ones. In this case, cables dropped from each of the skylights down to oversized mechanical wheels on each of the two floors overhead. From the looks of things, a few casual turns of each of the wheels raised the hatch of a corresponding skylight above.

Brick's gaze was following the path of one of those cables when a young man called to him from across the lobby.

"Can I help you, sir?"

Ransom shielded his eyes and saw a young guy, probably in his early 20s, who was stationed behind a massive steal counter. No doubt the assistant who had given him directions over the phone.

"Yes, I have an appointment with Ms. Alexander," Brick said.

"Detective Ransom?" the assistant confirmed as he walked around the edge of the counter.

"That's right."

Even Brick Ransom could see that this guy was attractive. He had *GQ* cover model looks, but just enough of a twinkle in his eye to let you know he hadn't just been the eye candy at college parties. He was no doubt quick-witted and a lady-killer. It was a good thing he was competing for women in a different age bracket or Ransom might have been in trouble.

"I'll take you up to Ms. Alexander's office."

The young man led Ransom around the corner and down a darkened hallway, where they stepped into an elevator cab that had been waiting with its doors open. A push of the button and the doors whisked closed.

"Did you find the building OK?"

"Piece of cake. Your directions got me here like-"

The doors popped open, revealing a totally different hallway.

"-the wind," Brick finished. "Wow."

Fast elevators were a sign of big money. Catacomb Press must be rolling in it.

"Ms. Alexander's office is to the right and down the hall. She's expecting you."

"Thanks," Brick said as he stepped out into the hallway.

Had they really gotten all the way to the top floor that quickly? A look down the corridor in the other direction showed the skylights were now a mere ten feet above him.

Impressive.

Between the Kundig building and the high-speed lift, Maureen Alexander's little upstart press was clearly playing with the big boys now.

He trod down the plushly carpeted hallway and stopped at a pair of thick glass doors. A peek inside revealed a slim, red-haired woman in a tailored suit and heels, who was leaning against a desk, reading a newspaper in the middle of a richly decorated office. Two leather sofas sat facing each other in the middle of the room. A steel coffee table sat between them. Just as Brick was lifting his hand to tap on the glass, the woman looked up and motioned for him to come inside.

"Detective Ransom, please come in," she said as she strode across the office, dropping the newspaper on the table as she stepped forward. "Maureen Alexander."

She'd crossed the room in what appeared to be four long strides. Brick glanced at her legs. She cut an athletic figure, most likely a runner, and though Brick knew she was just around 42 years of age, other than a pair of alluring laugh lines on either side of her mouth, she looked at *least* seven years younger.

"Thanks for taking the time to meet with me."

"Of course," Alexander said. A polite but busy smile flashed across her face.

She was an undeniably attractive woman, probably had been most her life. A few scars from adolescent skin problems offered the only hints that her path to adulthood might ever have been anything less that painless.

They shook hands while Brick pondered where to begin. He made a mental note to keep his train of thought strictly professional.

"Can I get you a cup of coffee?"

"No thank you. I've probably had too much already."

"I probably have too," she replied as she headed for a coffee maker that sat on a counter set into the wall behind her. "Unfortunately, I can't stop drinking the stuff."

"I know what you mean."

She filled a mug and motioned toward the couches as she headed over.

"Please, have a seat. I assume this is about Diane Norman's murder?"

"Yes, it is," Brick said as he sat down. "So, you know about that then…"

Alexander sat on the couch opposite him and kicked her foot toward the newspaper, which sat face up on the coffee table between them. Above a black and white file photo of Diane Norman, the headline read *'Bestselling Local Author Gunned Down.'*

"It was in the paper this morning."

"Oh, of course. It's funny, I get so caught up with my end

of the job that I forget most of this stuff gets reported in the paper as well."

"Most of it?" Alexander asked as she arched one eyebrow.

Brick smiled, "Well, hopefully all of it eventually, but we have to keep a few things under wraps from time to time till we've taken the right people into custody."

"It's still hard to believe," Alexander began. "I knew Diane for years. We basically started in this business together."

Brick glanced around the office, comparing the rather grandiose setting to the more modest atmosphere of Diane Norman's home.

"That's essentially the reason I'm here. From what we can gather, Ms. Norman wasn't exactly what you'd call a social butterfly-"

Maureen let out of knowing sigh. "No, that she was not."

"So, we're trying to piece things together a bit. See if we can develop a clear picture of her life in Seattle. Find reliable information that might point us in the right direction to identify her killer."

Alexander studied him over the top of her coffee cup as she took another sip. She set the drink down on top of the newspaper, and a splash of coffee washed over the edge, seeping around the sides of the cup and circling the exposed corners of Diane Norman's face. Brick watched the coffee ring expand across the damp newsprint.

"I suppose I'm as good a person as any to talk to," She began. "We've been on the outs for the last few years, but at one point I imagine I was the closest thing that woman had to family in this city."

"And how long did you say you knew Ms. Norman?"

"Well, I hate to admit this, but lets see. Her first book, *Sub Rosa,* was Catacomb's debut title, so that's means it was just under-" She hesitated. "Basically twenty years. That's a little scary."

"And you were friends?"

"Yes, we were very close for the first ten years or so, then things got-"

Brick waited for her to finish, but when she didn't, he stepped in.

"I take it the two of you had a falling out?"

Alexander nodded. "That's right."

"I ask because I spoke to a Mr. Ryan at-"

"Cryptic Bindings. I know Karl."

Brick smiled. "I didn't realize the Seattle book world was so closely knit. Well, Mr. Ryan indicated he'd seen you and Ms. Norman getting into a bit of a...*tête-à-tête* at an event last weekend. From what he said, I gather it became rather contentious."

"Oh. I forgot he was at that event. I'm sorry he had to see that. Yes, unfortunately, for the last few years it seems I wasn't able to bump into Diane Norman without her accusing me of some pecuniary misdeed or reviving yet another item on her long list of grievances."

"Can you give me some idea of what you mean by that?" Brick asked.

"I can try, but I have to tell you, I didn't believe her complaints ever had any merit, so I might not be faithfully reporting them the way she sees- well, saw them."

"Just the gist of it would be helpful."

Alexander picked up the cup again and sipped her coffee as she gathered her thoughts.

Brick looked from Alexander down to the ringed picture of the deceased author. His thoughts jumped back to the circle of frozen blood around Norman's body the day before.

"To put it as simply as possible, Diane left Catacomb Press for one of the New York publishers about five years ago, right around the time we started publishing a new author whose books were taking off *big time*. Diane felt, rightly so perhaps, that his books were… eclipsing her own. Unfortunately, it also seemed he was hitting a hot streak just as her own work was starting to tread water. Unfortunately, at last weekend's event she and our new author were paired up in a sort of joint reading slash Q and A. She took the opportunity presented by one audience member's question to launch into a tirade that was clearly an attack on our new star's work, and it went on from there."

"And was that author Dan Buckley?" Brick asked.

Alexander's eyes narrowed.

"Does it matter?"

"Just another puzzle piece to work with."

"Yes, it was Daniel Buckley."

"What kind of stuff does Mr. Buckley write?"

Alexander studied Brick for a moment. "You haven't read him? I'd think someone in your profession might really enjoy his work. He does a sort of contemporary pulp thing, like hard-boiled detective mysteries, but with a sense of humor, and more explicit details."

"And his books are doing well for you?" Brick asked.

"*Very* well. He's basically the reason this entire building is here. We discovered him and he's taken us along for the ride as his career has taken off. When she was still with Catacomb, Diane felt Daniel was getting too much of my time, too much of our marketing attention, too much of everything, so she cut her ties and jumped ship for one of the legacy imprints. That was just before she starting releasing a string of spectacularly unsuccessful books. Meanwhile, Daniel Buckley has only grown more successful with each new release. That really seemed to be eating at her. Even more than I had ever realized."

"Can you give me some examples?"

"The first time Dan Buckley hit the *New York Times'* bestseller list, Diane started hounding me. She claimed I owed her royalties on *Sub Rosa.* That I'd taken an unfair bite out of her profits over the years, that- well, honestly I couldn't really ever put all the pieces of her complaints against Catacomb Press and myself together. It all seemed so crazy that I finally just told her to have her lawyer call our legal and accounting department, and let *them* work it out 'cause I didn't know how to make her happy."

"And did it ever get resolved?" Brick asked.

Alexander shook her head. "No. She was completely unreasonable. And my business people could never see how we were anything but squared away and paid up with her. But that didn't keep her from bringing it up with me every time we crossed paths. It was exhausting. I feel cruel saying this, but she, like her books, just didn't make sense anymore. I don't think she even realized that her plots, her sentences even, just didn't fit together like they used to. Are you a reader, detective?"

"I go through spurts."

"Ever read D. J. Norman?"

"As a matter of fact, I just sampled my first D.J. Norman books last night."

"And what did you think?"

Brick inhaled deeply as he gathered his thoughts.

If she'd asked him to describe a dish, something like osso bucco, the words would likely have tumbled from his lips freely, but literature wasn't something he discussed everyday.

"Well, to be honest, I started with her new book first, but it...wasn't so great. I put it down and grabbed the first one. I'm about halfway done with that one."

"Then you know. *Sub Rosa* is a terrific book. It put us both on the map. And her other, earlier releases are quite good as well. It just seems like somewhere along the line, the blood in her ideas sort of... trickled away."

An unusual choice of words.

Brick stared at the floor as his mind again flashed to the crystalized puddle of blood that had surrounded Diane Norman's body.

"Do you recall what the two of you discussed at the event last weekend?"

"Well, it started with me confronting her about the cheap shots she'd taken at Daniel during the Q/A. Literally, cheap shots. *Cheap Thrills*... You see..."

Brick nodded.

"Daniel took the comments like a gentleman, but they were low blows. Insinuating there was something more to my relationship with him, that he was only successful because I'd taken him under my wing and sold the hell out of his stuff, in exchange for-"

"I think I get the picture," Brick said.

Alexander threw up her arms in concession. "I mean, what can you really say once you've denied that same charge from the same person time and again?"

"Was it true?" Brick asked.

Maureen Alexander's mouth grew tense at the corners for a moment before a bemused half smile crossed her lips. "No."

"I'm sorry for asking. And what else did you discuss?"

"From there, just the same stuff as always. It was the same old broken record. She was bitter about the poor sales of her new book, the one you tried to read last night. She wanted to know about her royalty payments for her back catalogue. I told her we were sending her everything she was entitled to. I mean, her old stuff still makes some money for us, but nowhere *near* what she must have been thinking. Then she started in on Daniel's stuff and took some swipes at the marketing efforts she thought we were giving to his books that she felt we'd never given to her titles-"

"Do you think she was right?"

"Comparatively, no. I mean, sure, we definitely spend more marketing a Daniel Buckley title than we ever spent on a D. J. Norman release, but with the amount of time that's gone by since we last handled one of Diane's titles… well, the book world has changed considerably since then. It simply takes more to get a book noticed. Plus, frankly, Daniel's books have made us more money in five years than her stuff brought in fifteen or even *twenty*. He's made this company vital in a way that it *never* was before."

"And how did you leave it?"

"She left it. She told me I'd be hearing from her lawyer yet again, then she stormed off to Karl Ryan's booth. Lord only knows what she must have said to him. Did he say?"

"They just made arrangements for her to come into his store to sign some books. Never ended up happening though."

"So, he didn't say anything about me?"

"Nothing pertinent," Brick replied. When he saw her expression, he elaborated. "He did comment about your business skills…"

"He called me cutthroat, didn't he?"

Brick nodded.

She smiled. "I love it, if I was a man they'd say I was a shrewd negotiator, but as a woman I'm always 'cutthroat and lack scruples.'"

"He didn't say anything about scruples."

Alexander narrowed her eyes at him, clearly unsure what to make of that comment. The two of them sat quietly for a moment as Brick ran the information through his head again.

Reading between the lines – and trying to keep his eyes off her legs – something in Alexander's manner made him uncomfortable.

"Did you see anyone else at this event? By the way, what was this thing called again?"

"'*Slash and Grab.*' It's a Northwest mystery event that happens every year."

"Did you see anyone else at this Slash and Grab thing who might have dealt with Ms. Norman or seen what happened?"

"Actually, I did see my former assistant as I was walking in, but other than that, I don't think any of us crossed paths."

"Us?"

"Me, Diane, or Daniel."

"Could I get her name?"

"Who?"

"Your former assistant. It might he helpful to speak with her."

"My former assistant is a man. Zack Baxter."

Did Maureen Alexander have a Joan Collins-style hiring policy when it came to assistants?

"And how long did he work for you?"

"He was with me for almost ten years. He left the company about six months ago."

"That's quite a long time to then fall completely out of touch," Brick observed. "Did things end amicably?"

"There were a few wrinkles in the separation."

Brick wasn't the least bit surprised.

"Would you be able to give me the numbers for Mr. Baxter and Daniel Buckley?"

"Of course," Alexander replied as she walked over to her desk. "I don't have Zack's information on hand, but my assistant can give it to you on your way out."

She opened a desk drawer and took out a Catacomb Press bookmark, on which she wrote Daniel Buckley's name and telephone number. Then she turned to the shelves of books behind her, took down a hardbound copy of Daniel Buckley's *Cheap* Thrills, and slipped the bookmark inside.

"As long as you're reading some of our titles, you might as well check out Daniel's latest. I think you'll enjoy it."

Brick crossed the room and accepted the book. "Thank you very much, I'm looking forward to it. And thank you for your time."

"I hope I've been of some help. Despite the unpleasant events the last few years, I really was sorry to hear about Diane."

Brick weighed the book in his hands as he held Maureen Alexander's unblinking gaze a moment longer. She really was a cool customer.

"We'll keep you posted," Brick said as he headed for the door. "Oh, can you tell me your assistant's name?"

"I told you. *Zack Baxter.*"

"No, I mean your *current* assistant."

She looked confused. "Oh, right. His name is Mike Attebery."

"Great, I'll get Baxter's contact information from Mike on my way out."

*   *   *

Brick was headed downtown, contemplating a detour to *Top Pot Doughnuts*, when Bob Seger started warbling from his coat pocket. He pulled out his phone and glanced at the caller ID: *Seattle P. I.*

Flynn.

He flipped on the hands-free speaker

"What can I do for you, Flynn?"

"Just letting you know I've given your number to Julie Price and told her to give you a call."

"Yeah, about that," Brick said as his thoughts drifted back to the Catacomb offices and Maureen Alexander's legs. "I'm thinking that might not be such a good idea after all."

"What a surprise," Flynn replied flatly.

"I was just thinking maybe-"

"Listen, Brick, I'm just letting you know I've given Julie your number. If you like, I can give you *hers* and you can sit on it, but I don't want to hear another long explanation for why you're no longer interested in giving this a chance. I've got to sign off and get back to work."

"Okay," Brick was a little taken aback. "I can see you're in a mood so-"

He was cut off by the sound of the call disconnecting.

"Hello? *Hello?*"

Flynn had hung up on him.

That was new.

It made Brick mad.

* * *

Brick dumped the two D. J. Norman titles and Daniel Buckley's latest on his desk, along with a half-loaf of the bread he'd baked the night before.

O'Brien looked up his from his computer at the sound of the commotion. Their desks faced one another, giving him a front row seat as Brick worked, or attempted to work. O'Brien studied the pile of food and literature closely.

"You've been busy, I see. Did you happen to do anything related to our investigation since I saw you last?"

Brick gave him a look. "As a matter of fact, yeah. I was just speaking to D.J. Norman's publisher." He ripped a corner of bread from the loaf and stuffed it in his mouth. "And judging from your attitude, I take it you don't want any of my bread," he mumbled as he struggled to chew, all too aware of how bratty he'd just sounded.

O'Brien hesitated, then put out his hand. Brick tossed him the bulk of the loaf.

"Did her publisher have anything to offer?"

Brick flipped his computer on and took a seat while he waited for the screen to flash on.

"Possibly. What have you found out?"

"Nothing that'll crack the case."

"Any word from Anna on cause of death?"

"Yeah, two bullets," O'Brien said, deadpan, "Not like we didn't know *that* already."

"Could this computer be any slower?" Brick grumbled as

he slapped the side of his monitor. The screen flickered off, then on again, then it went black. He slapped it once more and the startup screen blinked on.

"You know Metzger hates it when you do that."

Brick shrugged. He was all too familiar with their IT guy's intolerance for his computer-smacking ways. He picked up Daniel Buckley's book and pulled out the bookmark. He looked at the number Maureen Alexander had jotted down, then he grabbed his cell and punched it in.

Voicemail.

He waited for the greeting to play out, then launched into his message. "Good evening, Mr. Buckley. This is Detective Brick Ransom with the Seattle Police Department. Could you please give me a call at your earliest convenience? My number is (206) 327-7198."

Ransom hung up the phone and looked at his computer, which was finally loading a Windows screen. He dug through his pockets and took out another sheet of paper on which Alexander's latest boy toy of an assistant had scrawled Zack Baxter's number in almost illegible handwriting.

The phone rang, Bob Seger's voice triggering an involuntary cringing motion from O'Brien's side of the desk

Brick's eyes darted to the readout, which again read: *Seattle P. I.*

"I gotta tell you, that is the *worst* ringtone I have *ever* heard," O'Brien exclaimed.

"Yeah, sorry, my nephew put it on there."

He'd actually set it up himself after a few White Russians and one misguided viewing of 'Beverly Hills Cop II.'

Brick answered the call, immediately launching into a mini tirade, "Yeah, Flynn, thanks for hanging up on me earlier. I was thinking about it, and the last thing I want to do is get set up on a blind date with some film geek social pariah you work with, so why don't we just-"

He stopped short.

"Oh, Julie," Brick said. "Sorry, I uh, thought it was Flynn playing another one of his pranks. No, not at all, I was talking about… it's a long story."

O'Brien set his feet up on his desk and drew his hands back behind his head as he settled in for the show

"No, no. I mean *yes*, of course I'd like to go to dinner sometime." Brick nodded. "Tomorrow would be perfect. Can you give me your number in case I need to call you back outside of your work?"

Brick nodded some more as he jotted her information down and tried to ignore O'Brien's smirk.

"That would be perfect, it's one of my favorites actually. Looking forward to it."

He hung up the phone and looked over at O'Brien, who was chewing on a hunk of bread and flashing a Cheshire cat grin.

"You are *quite* the charmer this morning," O'Brien said with a laugh.

Brick slapped his hand to his forehead. "I am definitely off my game, man." He reached out his hands and O'Brien tossed the loaf back to him. Brick tore off another piece and flipped through Buckley's latest book.

"You ever read anything by Daniel Buckley?"

"Me, nah. Should I?"

Brick pulled up the Amazon page for *Cheap Thrills* and scanned the reviews as he dialed Zack Baxter's number.

Voicemail again.

He covered the mouthpiece, "Doesn't anybody answer the phone anymore?"

O'Brien shrugged.

Brick looked at some of the reviews on the page as he waited for the greeting to play out. His eyes settled on one entitled: *"Hackneyed writing, ridiculous story."* Brick skimmed the angry little tirade. *"Trite characters, absurd plot, action that is simply beyond the pale. If you have time to kill in a waiting room before a colonoscopy, as I did, then I suppose there are worse books out there."*

"What a cockmonkey!" Brick exclaimed.

O'Brien looked around the room, then tried to shush him.

"These people, man!" Ransom exclaimed.

Baxter's greeting ended.

"Hello, Mr. Baxter, this is Officer Ransom from the Seattle Police Department. I wonder if you might-"

The phone clicked, the sound on the line shifting as someone picked up the call midway through his message.

"Hello?" Ransom asked. "Is this Zack Baxter? Yes. I'm calling in regard to an ongoing homicide investigation, and your former employer gave me your name as someone who might have information about a Ms. Diane Norman-"

Ransom listened to Baxter's response and gave O'Brien the thumbs up.

"If you have time today that would be-" Brick stopped and looked at his watch as he grabbed a pen. "Noon would be perfect. If I can get your address I'll head right over."

*   *   *

"I'm surprised Maureen gave you my number. I thought they were doing everything they could to keep me out of

Dan's orbit."

The comment caught Brick by surprise.

"By Dan, do you mean Daniel Buckley?" Ransom asked.

"Yeah, who else would I be talking about?" Baxter asked.

Ransom leaned back in the IKEA dining chair. The curved wooden back creaked under his weight.

He had left the office as soon as he'd hung up the phone, and had driven directly to Capitol Hill. Zack Baxter lived in The Madison Lofts, an old warehouse and manufacturing building that had been converted into condos, complete with a wall of old industrial sewing machines in the lobby, thick wooden beams, and the type of exposed brick walls that would make a *Sunset Magazine* editor blush, even as she stroked the grout longingly. Brick couldn't help but let out a slow whistle as he crossed the lobby's creaking, wide-planked floor. Everything about this place spoke of money, privilege, self-pampering, and conspicuous consumption. All with that distinct Northwest minimalist conceit. In short, the place was *incredible,* and Brick was having a hell of a time figuring how a guy Baxter's age was able to afford it. It didn't matter how much he might have saved by getting his furniture at IKEA, the building and its subsequent lifestyle were clearly out of the financial reach of a former publishing assistant turned, apparently, one-off literary event coordinator.

Baxter seemed reasonably friendly. Just this side of 30, with a tall, solid build, the kind that could fill out a suit, but would never require him to wear ribbed V-necks and kiss his biceps. Ransom was starting to understand why Maureen Alexander had originally hired him.

"Mr. Baxter, this isn't about Dan Buckley, it's about D.J. Norman. You might have seen she was shot to death yesterday morning?"

"Of course. I saw the story in the paper. That was just… weird."

"'Weird' how, if you don't mind my asking?" Ransom said as he leaned forward uncomfortably.

These Swedish dining chairs never had enough padding.

Brick studied Baxter's hands as the younger man rested them on the table for a moment. They had the slightest tremor to them, which, perhaps unconsciously, he seemed to compensate for by keeping them always in motion. On closer inspection, he also had what Brick found to be a rather off-putting smirk, a full-on grin that flashed across his face from time to time, usually when Brick was just beginning to look away. It was the look of someone who knew something, but didn't want to let you in on the secret, like you had something embarrassing stuck to the seat of your pants, but he wouldn't pay you the courtesy of letting you know that it was there.

"It was a strange coincidence is all," Baxter said. "I just saw that lady for the first time in years at an event I worked on last weekend."

"Slash and Grab?"

Baxter nodded. "I used to see her all the time when I worked for Maureen, but it had been ages since I'd laid eyes on her. Then, a couple days after I see her again, she's on the front page of the paper. Dead."

"Did you speak with her last weekend?"

"No way," Zack replied. "After the way she laid into Dan during their Q and A, I figured if she even recognized me she'd just let me have it too. I didn't want anything to do with her. She seemed to have a beef with everyone who had ever worked at Catacomb."

"You're actually the third person to mention her appearance with Mr. Buckley. Can you tell me a little bit about what happened?"

"Well, where to begin? You know she had a grudge with him, right?"

Brick half-nodded, half-grimaced.

His ass was starting to kill him from this damn chair.

"I made that pretty clear to the folks running Slash and Grab. I understood they'd both started out at the same press, and they'd both released new titles in the last couple of weeks, but having them do a joint reading and audience Q and A seemed like a very bad idea to me."

"And it sounds like it was."

"Definitely wasn't pretty. They were both up on the stage, each at their own little lectern, reading excerpts in front of an audience. Some professor from UW, I forget his name, Professor Flannelknob or something, was doing a real half-assed job running the thing. He'd point to them to let them know when to talk, but he wouldn't step in when Norman would turn attack dog. During the question and answer session, he just sort of handed off the mics and let her rip into Dan's stuff over and over. It was really crazy when you consider that even *now* the guy is a hundred times the writer she *ever* was."

"Even now?" Brick quoted back to him.

"Well, I suppose I do have one foot slightly in the camp of the readers who feel Dan's style has changed a bit from his earlier books. But he's still one of the best pulp writers publishing today. The things Diane was spouting were completely out to lunch."

"Can you give me some examples?" Brick asked.

"To be honest, it's all kind of whirled together in my mind. I like Dan, we used to be pretty close actually, so I took her attacks personally. Sure, he's streamlined his approach a bit, but his plots are still as tight as hell. 'Course he just shrugs that kind of criticism off anyways and keeps working. But that lady is too much. She seemed to find a way to claim everything *good* about the current mystery scene was her doing, and everything *bad* was reflected in the success of writers like Daniel Buckley."

Brick stood up.

He couldn't take the chair anymore.

"How would you describe Buckley's books? Who reads them?"

"He's a throwback to the hard-boiled masters," Baxter said. "Folks who dig the classics *love* Dan Buckley books."

Brick walked over to the wall of windows. The sill was covered with hardbound and paperback books. He noticed quite a few of the titles were Buckley's. The rest included stuff from Raymond Chandler, Dashiell Hammett, and James M. Cain.

"You must really be a fan of the genre then."

"If you ask me, it's the purest form of fiction. Clear structure, classic entertainment, no bullshit motivations. It's not like literary fiction, where something can be a purple, preposterous mess, and everyone falls over themselves praising it, even if they don't know what it's about or it fails completely. Hard-boiled fiction either works, or it doesn't, and when it does, it's some of the sharpest, most stylish writing there is."

"And you really think Dan Buckley is as good as these

guys?" Brick asked as he ran his fingers over the spines of the books on the windowsill.

"He absolutely is," Baxter grunted. "If he can keep up the sales and get a little closer to the gritty style of his first few books, the ones that weren't such guaranteed bestsellers, he could be one of the greatest mystery writers of all time."

"That's a hell of a statement. What do you mean about getting back to the style of his earlier books?"

Baxter shrugged his shoulders with a smirk. "I guess it's normal when a writer starts to enjoy mainstream success, but a lot of his fans, I suppose myself included, have noticed that as his books come out at a faster clip, the details seem to be a little less..." Baxter searched for the words and started again. "It just feels like he's sanding the corners down a little too much. The motives aren't as black and white, the killings aren't as primal, and the language feels...airbrushed. Don't get me wrong. I still love everything he puts out, but if you pressed me, I suppose I'd admit that the latest book in particular strikes me as being a little... bloodless."

"And you think that's because he's aiming for a broader audience?"

"I guess I do," Baxter said. "He's socializing with people in the Seattle society scene now. I suspect he wants to make more money so he can try to keep up with the Puget Sound software millionaires, and unless David Fincher turns around and makes one of his earlier books into a movie, Dan probably thinks he needs to make his stuff a little less controversial in order to be a regular read on the jet-set circuit."

"Interesting. You're the first person I've spoken to who has said that."

"Then talk to some other fans. I know I'm not the only one who thinks it. Now, that being said, I stand by my earlier comments, he's *still* better than 80 percent of the mystery writers working today, and he's a thousand times better than D.J. Norman ever was, even in her prime."

Brick glanced out the window as he gathered his thoughts. Baxter's condo faced west, and he could just see the front of The Elliot Bay Book Company. No wonder Baxter lived in this neighborhood.

He wondered again who might be picking up the tab for this primo condo.

"Do you know Karl Ryan at Cryptic Bindings?" Brick asked.

"I've met him. Been in his store quite a few times, but that's about the scope of it."

"Ryan said he observed a pretty heated confrontation involving Maureen Alexander and Diane Norman that took place after the event. Did you happen to see that as well?"

"I didn't see it. I sort of keep my distance from Maureen after the way things ended, but I'd certainly believe it. Those two were *always* getting into it when I worked there."

Ransom turned away from the window and walked back to the table. Along the way he passed a side table covered with a half-dozen copies of *McSweeney's* literary journal. That struck him as a bit off. He'd dated a UW grad-student a few years back, Carley. Cute girl. Lot of fun. But she'd taken a hell of a long time to get ready every time they went out. She'd been a big *McSweeney's* fan, so over time Brick had flipped through quite a few editions of that literary journal while he was waiting for her to wrap things up. He'd found that each and every page of that publication had the uncanny ability to bring to mind a different four-letter word, the most frequent being "twee" and "smug." If any journal seemed antithetical to hard-boiled fiction, it was the published collections from Dave Eggers' quirk-factory *McSweeney's*.

"I hope you don't mind me asking a sort of rude question, but did anything *personal* ever occur between you and Ms. Alexander?"

Baxter laughed. "Personal? Nice term. No, I think she might have hired me for that, but she was into some sort of… different stuff than me."

Brick filed that comment away as well.

"So then, why did you stop working for her?"

Baxter took a moment to chew that question over.

"She thought I was too intensely focused on the writers and not as interested in the office work." Baxter shrugged. "She was probably right, but she sure could have ended it better."

Brick felt his phone vibrate in his pocket. He'd flipped off the sound. The last thing he needed while conducting an interview was for Bob Seger's *Shakedown* to derail the conversation.

"And you worked for Catacomb for ten years?"

"That's right," Baxter said. "Ten years, with about five minutes notice before Maureen threw me out. Said I needed to remember my place at the company. Lady is cutthroat"

"Funny how often the same words keep coming up in this case. What did she mean by 'remember your place' at the company?"

"Maureen likes the people she works with to be fairly submissive." He gave Brick a look. "You met with Dan?"

Brick shook his head as he took his phone from his

pocket and glanced at the screen. Dan Buckley's number appeared under *missed calls.*

"I haven't spoken with him yet, but I think it's time I did."

*   *   *

One of these days, Brick knew his car would no longer have the power to make it up the hills to Queen Anne. Then he'd have to trade in his father's old cruiser and let the department assign him one of their newer, supposedly more reliable models. He'd hate to see the old man's vehicle taken off the road; as long as it was still out there working cases, it felt like Curt Ransom was alive and well and prowling the city. Fortunately, today was not the day the old car threw in the towel, and though the boxy white monstrosity squealed a bit as its tires dug into the asphalt on the counterbalance, it eventually made it up to the top, where it once again handled like a charm.

Ransom had returned Dan Buckley's call as he walked back to his car. He'd just finished his work for the day, and would be free to talk over the next few hours, so Brick had jotted down the address and hurried over.

Buckley's place was the stuff Emerald City dreams were made of. The view alone would have made Frasier jealous. As for the design, it gave even Maureen Alexander's freshly erected Kundig masterpiece a run for its money. If Alexander had seen Buckley's place, which she no doubt had, she probably wanted one of her own.

Brick pulled up to the front of the two-story steel and glass home. The driveway was composed of perforated honeycomb panels, with patches of densely packed earth pressed into the gaps. A thick layer of finely trimmed grass sprouted from the packed soil. It was one of those low-impact, concrete-alternative driveways, the kind that let the rain pass through without disrupting the water table below. Apparently Daniel Buckley was both a best-selling author and a walk-the-talk environmentalist. Either that, or the house had come that way. Curiously, the home didn't have a garage. In fact, there didn't appear to be any sort of vehicle in sight. Maybe that was an environmental decision as well.

Brick parked near the end of the driveway, hoping to hell the cruiser didn't leak oil and kill the grass. He shut the door and headed towards the house, listening to the scrape of the perforated paving stones clinking together as he crossed them. With all the recent snow and rain, the panels made a subtle sloshing sound underfoot as he made his way to the front door and rang the bell. A reverberant gonging sound echoed from the back, and a few moments later the door swung open, revealing a boyishly handsome 38-year-old. Buckley was about five foot nine, with a head of salt and pepper hair and a funny little half grin that rested beneath serious, pinched eyebrows. Brick recognized him from the author photo on the back of *Cheap Thrills*.

"Detective Ransom," he said as he put out his hand. "Dan Buckley. Please come in."

"Pleasure meeting you. I appreciate you taking the time out of your day."

"Are you kidding?" Buckley said as he led the way. "I'm a mystery writer. I couldn't dream of a better opportunity to see how things are *really* done. Might help me sidestep some mistakes next time."

An interesting comment, given the circumstances.

Brick knew he was referring to his next book, but he

made a mental note of it all the same. He also made note of the hand-carved cherry flooring that ran throughout the house. Gorgeous.

He needed to find a better-paying gig so he good upgrade his lifestyle!

Buckley led Brick down a long, dark entryway, then up two steps, till they were standing in a glass-and-steel enclosed living room that looked out over downtown Seattle. The Space Needle glimmered in the foreground beneath the afternoon sun.

"You have an amazing home."

"Thank you. Can I get you something to drink?"

"Might as well just get started," Brick said.

Buckley motioned to the living room, where they each took a seat, with Brick still facing the city through the wall of glass. The couches had that overstuffed feeling to them that Brick had come to associate with money. In his years sitting and interviewing sources, he'd found that rich folks, no matter the background, favored at least three of the same things: hurricane lanterns, gunite swimming pools, and big-ass couches. Yet, unlike the vast majority of the sofas on which he'd questioned witnesses, this couch was actually *comfortable*. He'd be willing to bet Dan Buckley had picked it out himself, rather than deferring to some bony-assed interior designer. It certainly beat the hell out of Zack Baxter's IKEA chairs.

Brick turned his attention to the skyline. "Lot of people in this city would kill for that view."

"So they tell me," Buckley said. "I guess my characters have killed to get it for me."

"What's that hill like in the winter? Day like yesterday, I

imagine you were stuck inside all day."

"I wouldn't know actually. I don't drive. Grew up in Manhattan and never had a reason to learn. Besides, with my profession, being stuck inside is often a good thing, makes it harder to put off getting to work." Buckley pointed over his shoulder to the end of the long, steel table that sat in the middle of an open dining room; a laptop sat at the head. Brick noticed three enormous glass hurricane lanterns evenly spaced down the middle. "The snow just gave me more time to work on my first draft."

"How long have you lived in Seattle?" Ransom asked.

"About seven years."

"And you never have trouble getting where you want to go? Even up here on the hill?"

Buckley shook his head. "I have drivers, and you'd be amazed how many places deliver. If I ever want to get somewhere right away, I just hop on the bus."

"Well, you're a better man than me."

Buckley smiled, but it was clear he was ready to get on with the discussion.

"Now, what can I do for you, Detective Ransom?"

"Well, like I mentioned on the phone, we're looking into the death of Diane Norman."

"Such a terrible thing. I still can't believe it," Buckley said.

Ransom nodded, watching his expression coolly.

"Can I ask you something, Mr. Buckley?"

"Sure. And please, you can call me Dan."

Brick nodded politely, but held off on the familiarity, "So far as you know, other than Maureen Alexander, did anyone at Catacomb Press have bad blood with Ms. Norman?"

Buckley exhaled heavily. "I don't know that I'd call it bad blood, but pretty much everyone I know had run-ins with her. She had a chip on her shoulder. It was common knowledge that she saw herself as the company's star, and when Maureen started expanding the scope of the author roster and some newer names started doing pretty well, it seemed like Diane took it as an affront... Not to sound obnoxious, but she probably had the most complaints with me-"

"Because you were the most successful of the bunch?" Brick asked.

Buckley nodded. "I think so. And boy did Diane ever make it clear she felt *she* was the better writer, and that my books wouldn't have been selling the way they were without Maureen putting everything she had into pushing them."

"And do you think that's true?"

"Of course not. I mean, Maureen did help to make my titles successful; but she put the same amount of energy into plugging my stuff as she did with the books of everyone else she publishes. She didn't play favorites. God knows she certainly threw too *much* money at the last few D.J. Norman releases before Diane signed on with the boys in New York."

"By 'boys' you mean the publishing houses back East?" Brick asked.

"Yes."

"And was Maureen mad about that?"

"About Diane's accusations, or about the jump to the old-school pubs?"

"Both."

"To tell you the truth, I think Maureen was relieved to be rid of her." Buckley held Ransom in his gaze. "You've probably heard that she and Maureen had their blow-ups, but that wasn't an entirely new thing. Up until a few years ago, they were like sisters, dysfunctional, vindictive sisters, but sisters nonetheless. I know a thing or two about the subject, I've got a few of them myself, and from what I've seen from a distance, they interact in their own little world, separate from the rest of the family. It was the same with Maureen and Diane."

"So they were close. What changed it?"

"What always changes any relationships?" Buckley asked as he rubbed his middle and index fingers against his thumb. "Money: Before she signed elsewhere, Diane wanted more of it, and Maureen felt she had run out of it to give her. Maureen told me she'd placed her bets on the same hand too many times, and felt she had to cut her losses."

"But before that, they were really close?"

"Extremely. Neither one of them had much in the way of family out here. And they'd met during their respective salad days, so even after the falling out, those roots went *deep*. Even when things were at their most strained for the last couple of years, I'd still have pitied any outsider that got between the two of them."

"Did *you* ever get caught in the middle?"

"Not directly, but I know my climbing sales caused Maureen some headaches every time Diane wanted to talk numbers and logistics. D. J. Norman did *not* like to share resources."

"Would you say Ms. Norman was a bit of a diva?"

"Probably, but God love her, Maureen Alexander is more than her equal. She's a self-made woman, and she'll definitely let you know it."

"You ever seen the two of them go head to head?"

Buckley nodded. "Once or twice. I clearly remember showing up one time at the tail-end of a Diane vs. Maureen blowout at the old building. I got there early for my own meeting, and sat in the waiting room outside Maureen's door as the two of them had it out. Maureen's assistant and I definitely heard an earful before Diane stormed out."

"Was that assistant Zack Baxter?"

"It was."

"I was just speaking to Zack this morning."

"Really? I've wondered how he was doing since he left. Few years ago the two of us were starting to become friends, but it went sour. I'm sure he blamed me for his troubles with Maureen."

"Was he liked around the company? He ever deal with Diane?"

"I'm *sure* he dealt with Diane. He worked with Maureen longer than almost anyone *but* Diane." Buckley leaned back in his chair as he gathered his thoughts. "As for being liked around the company. Like I said, I was friends with him, briefly, but I know some of the other writers, not to mention his coworkers, felt he didn't really carry his own weight. And yeah, he probably wasn't the best publishing assistant."

"Would you say he was…what? Lazy?"

"In his office job? No. Just…erratic, and disorganized, and fairly unreliable."

Brick had to laugh. "Sounds like a great employee!"

"Yeah, now that I think about it, he managed to piss off just about everyone at one point or another," Buckley conceded. "But, I think I know where he was coming from. He went to some very good universities in Colorado, attended

I don't know how many publishing workshops around the country. He stuck with Maureen for eons on a paltry salary, then she let him go with damn near nothing to show for his years at the press that would give him a leg-up at his next gig."

"What do you suppose he expected from her?"

"Well for one thing, I think he was hoping she'd give him a chance to do something more than just answer phones and handle administrative tasks. He wanted to work with the writers and develop books. That was his passion, not his *own* writing, but helping others with their craft. He definitely wanted to be an editor and publisher in the Maureen Alexander mode. To be honest, I still don't know if he was well suited to that type of work, which is sort of tragic in its way. But he certainly felt he knew what was best for everyone else's stuff."

"He ever give you any advice?" Brick asked.

"Funny enough, yeah. I think I'm the only author Maureen gave him a shot at working with closely. He helped me prep the final draft of my second book."

"And how did that go?"

Buckley let out a sigh.

"Total disaster. He gave me a few insights that improved the work, but ultimately, I couldn't finish it with him."

"What was the problem?"

"He thought he knew better about *everything,* and he got mad if you didn't revise things exactly his way. He was a terrifying perfectionist. He wanted to fight it out over any change I made to the text, and if I didn't make a change, then he wanted to battle back and forth over the changes I *didn't* make as well. Eventually it was just too much pressure.

Exhausting actually."

"Exhausting for him?"

"Exhausting for *me*," Buckley admitted. "It squeezed every drop of fun out of the experience. Seemed like every decision I made broke his heart, or set him on edge, or made him think of a whole *other* direction I should be taking the book. I think he saw it as his one shot before the gate might close on him. That's part of why I stuck with it for as long as I could stand it, but I finally asked Maureen if she could have him work with someone else. Instead, she just stuck him back behind the reception desk. Like I said, he soured on me after that. My second book wasn't nearly as successful as the first, and I'm certain he felt it would have done better if I'd continued working on the manuscript with him. Finally, he turned on me. There's a fine line between adoration and hatred, and he went dark. When my third book was a blockbuster with zero involvement on his part, he turned nasty. That's when Maureen fired him."

"Any idea how he took that?"

"The firing? He took it," Buckley said. "I love her, but Maureen Alexander has a convincing way of making acceptance a person's only option. If anything, I think he held it against *me* more than anyone else."

"Friends to enemies. Why is that so often the way?"

Buckley shrugged. "The line between adoration and hatred is razor thin."

"And he never worked with anyone else at Catacomb? Ms. Alexander didn't set him up with Diane Norman to see if he could get her books back on the rails?"

"Detective, I know you didn't ever meet her, but you must be forming some sort of picture of Diane Norman by now. Do you really think that *she* of all people would have been willing to consider the guidance of a development editor in his mid-20s?

"I suppose you're right. Did you ever hear anything more from Baxter after he left the company? When was that, by the way?"

"Maureen canned him midway through last year. Actually, I did get a note from Zack a couple months ago when *Cheap Thrills* first came out. He gave me a fairly enthusiastic assessment of it, and suggested a couple of scenarios for my follow-up."

"You gonna take em?"

Buckley raised an eyebrow. "We'll see."

"You feel like he's forgiven you?"

"I guess I did, yeah. I mean, I certainly hope he has. He's a good guy, even if I couldn't bear the thought of ever working with him again."

Brick leaned back, rifling through his mental notes, seeing if there was anything he had missed. He seemed to have covered it. Better to leave more specific questions, like whether Buckley owned a firearm, until a later date. Fact-finding missions were sensitive procedures, no sense pulling the trigger just yet.

Brick rose to his feet and Buckley did likewise. Ransom handed him one of his business cards. "Thank you again for your time." He glanced over Buckley's shoulder and noticed what appeared to be a gunite lap pool visible through the dining room window. "If you think of anything else, please don't hesitate to give me a call."

* * *

Brick barely had time to get home and get changed. He

was due at the Dahlia Lounge at 7:00 for his date with Julie Price, but with fix-ups he always liked to get to the place early for a warm-up drink at the bar; his attempt to relax a bit before acting instantaneously forthcoming. Aside from one occasion, when his date had been late, and he'd indulged in four sidecars too many and turned zombie, it usually helped him let his guard down and have a nominally good time.

Ransom straightened his shirt, made sure the buttons lined up with the fly of his pants, ran a comb through his hair, and headed out the door. He was trudging down The Dean's staircase when his phone rang.

O'Brien's name appeared on the screen.

Brick answered as he slipped out the front door en route to his car.

"What's the latest?" he asked as he pulled his jacket closed and headed down the street.

The temperature had dropped again. Darkening storm clouds were moving in overhead. They might be in for more winter weather tonight.

This girl had better be worth the trouble.

"I looked into Norman's family situation. Never married. No kids, not even undeclared ones. She has a sister in Chicago, but there's no real motive there. The lady is rich."

"Rich like how rich?"

"Rich like *"she married the heir to a classic condiment empire"*-rich. Like, *"the family business is inheriting and managing the family fortune"*-rich."

"But Norman didn't come from that kind of money, right? Think there's any possibility of a 'get her before she gets me' kind of thing between them?" Brick asked as he unlocked his car and settled in behind the wheel.

"Like the sister had her killed to protect her fortune? Doesn't seem likely, man. The sister is married, happily, with plenty of kids and lots of fundraising events around Chicago to keep her busy. Google her if you ever want to feel socially inconsequential. Only folks who would benefit from her kicking it would be her children, her husband, and a half-dozen Chicago non-profits. Looks like a dead end if you ask me. Pardon the pun."

"All right, well, thanks for checking. I spoke with Buckley after I left Baxter's. Not sure what to think of that. He didn't strike me as the type to hold a grudge. Might want to look into the history between Diane and Maureen Alexander a little closer though. That strikes me as a potential sisterly-slaying type of scenario."

"Funny you should mention that. I checked on Alexander too. Turns out she's a registered gun owner with a concealed carry permit."

"You're kidding."

Brick rested his hands on the steering wheel as he processed that information. He pictured Alexander leaning against her desk reading as he came into the office that morning. Yeah, he could see her wearing those heels and a dangly little shoulder holster-

Mmmmm...

"You still there?" O'Brien asked.

"Yeah, just thinking. Be interesting to learn the background on that carry permit."

"Then I will do some more digging in regards to Ms. Alexander."

"Any other updates from Anne?"

"Nope."

Brick turned the ignition and the engine grumbled to life.

"All right, well, lets call it a night."

"You heading' out for your date?"

"Yeah, hoping I have time to fit in a liquid courage appetizer."

O'Brien laughed. "Ah, the life of the single 30-something. I don't miss it."

"Thanks a lot!"

"Seriously," O'Brien said. "Have a good one."

"Thank you," Brick said, worried his appreciation would echo through his voice a little *too* loud and clear; he was touched his partner seemed to care.

*   *   *

By the time he'd parked his car in the lot at 3rd and Virginia, the snow was really coming down. Brick had to watch his footing closely as he strolled down the sidewalk to the Dahlia Lounge. The dinner crowd was out in force as he entered. A few early arrivals were sitting on the front benches near the maître d' station. Julie had made the reservation for 7:00, which gave him 25 minutes to savor a manhattan at the bar and brace himself for the worst.

He nodded to the hostess, who recognized him on sight, but didn't ask for his name. She was probably used to seeing him make a beeline for the bar whenever he met Flynn there for happy hour. Brick headed that way now as well.

The dread was setting in.

Why in the hell had he broken his fix-up rule and let Flynn play matchmaker? He had strict policies when it came to blind dates, especially when it came to blind dates with his friends' *coworkers*. Any wrong move had the potential to haunt him for years.

So, what made this situation any different? Why had Flynn, who never tried to fix him up, decided this was a good time to give it a shot? And why had Brick gone for it? Well, for one thing, his own efforts at meeting someone were starting to seem a wee bit… pathetic. For another, he had strict policies on a lot of things, and what good had those done him? A one-bedroom bachelor pad and a lot of quiet nights alone? He couldn't even commit to a pet.

Hey now, don't go to a dark place. Tonight could be a pivot point.

He was out now, in the throbbing heart of the city. He'd opened himself up to the unknown, time to go with it and see where the evening took him. For all he knew this girl could be Ms. Right.

He headed toward the counter, his eyes scanning the room till they settled on a woman at the bar who was twirling her hair in her fingers with one hand, and running an index finger along the rim of a cocktail glass with the other. He couldn't get a good look at her face, but the angle of that wrist, and the way her crossed legs filled out those jeans…

Brick increased his stride.

If the date didn't work out, maybe this prospect could be Ms. Right.

She was seated at the corner, sipping from what appeared to be a healthy pour of scotch. Neat. Fortunately for him, the counter was crowded, but a couple of seats were still open. Even better, one of them was at a perfect 90-degree angle from the hair-twirling tippler.

Brick took a seat and tried to act mysterious, which is

to say, he tried not to get caught looking at her. He did, however, sneak a peak at the clock behind the bar. 15 minutes before Julie Price was due to arrive, that left him plenty of time to jam a wedge in the window of opportunity with this scotch-quaffing siren here, and still polish off his drink and greet his fix-up like a gentleman, albeit a gentleman with one eye locked on the gorgeous woman across the room.

Rene, the bartender, came over to take his order. From the frequency with which Brick and Flynn took advantage of the *P.I.'s* account with the restaurant, Rene knew him by name.

"What can I get for you, Brick? More of that mother's milk?" Rene asked with a smirk.

Brick wanted to kick himself.

Why in the hell had he jokingly called his White Russians 'mother's milk' the last time he was in here?

"No, I think I'll skip the *White Russian* this time and go with my old fallback, Rene."

There, that had had a breezy, Sinatra-like swing to it, right? Perfect recovery.

"Your fallback..." Rene looked at him blankly. "Not *mother's milk?*"

Brick's eyes darted over to the woman, who was playing with the swizzle stick in her drink now. God, she was gorgeous. Unfortunately, the corner of her mouth was also pulling up in the corner just a bit, like she was stifling a smile.

She was listening. Dammit.

"No, Rene. Not mother's milk!" Brick said again, a tinge of panic slipping into his voice. "A manhattan, that's my fallback. A manhattan."

Rene saw Brick's eyes dart in the woman's direction. Now he had a little half-smile on his face too.

"Oh, right-right-right. Yeah, I'll have that for you in a jiffy," Rene laughed.

He was messing with him. And Brick had of course fallen for it.

Ransom's hand fidgeted on the edge of the bar as he pondered his opening line. He needed to come up with something smooth. Something that was both off-the-cuff casual, but allowed for a nice ongoing discussion. He'd just settled on a question about the woman's scotch of choice, when he glanced over and saw she was looking right at him. Her eyes were a hypnotic pale blue.

Brick's mouth went dry.

"I'm a White Russian fan myself," she said with a grin.

He could feel his face growing warm. He hoped like hell his cheeks weren't turning red.

"Yeah. They're a classic," he said. "I knew I shouldn't have made that mother's milk joke last time. Rene likes to tease me, but I guess they're not exactly manly."

She picked up her drink. "Who cares? Men need mother's milk just like everyone else…"

Boy. Did they ever.

She took a long, slow drink. Brick stared at her lips as they pressed against the edge of the glass, leaving the faintest kiss of lipstick on the crystal before they pulled away, still glistening with alcohol.

"That's true." Brick swallowed hard. "That's very true."

Keep it together, Ransom.

He studied her for a moment. Now that he had a front row seat, he could see just how attractive this woman was.

She was a knockout. Long, light-brown hair, with just a hint of blond highlights. Sort of a dusty blond. He'd guess she was 30, with a youthful glow countered by the lean beauty of a maturing woman. Her features had a distinct Jennifer Aniston quality, but with slightly darker brows and a distinctly mischievous smile, which she flashed in Brick's direction again as he nodded his head, grasping for the next word as he snuck a peek at the clock.

6:47. Dammit. Soon he'd have to cut this short and sit on the bench and wait for stupid Julie Price.

"Now, that's a respectable drink you have there. What is that?"

She raised her glass and Brick noticed she wasn't wearing a ring.

"Dalwhinnie," she said

Brick nodded. Sounded strong.

"Would you like a sip?"

He glanced at the front door. The coast seemed clear.

"Sure, why not?"

He leaned closer as she set the glass on the counter and slid it over to him. Then he snatched it up and took a quick gulp. He immediately choked.

Dear God.

He slid the glass back and clamped his lips shut. Tight. But it was no use. Brick let out a long wheeze, just managing to swallow the mouthful of burning hell before he coughed painfully.

Rene looked at him from the far end of the bar.

This was humiliating.

He looked sheepishly in his neighbor's direction. She was smiling, but it didn't have the smirking quality he had dreaded seeing. If anything, there was an extra twinkle in her eyes now.

"You okay?"

He swallowed. "Yeah. Yeah. Phew, must have gone down the wrong pipe."

"It takes some getting used to."

Rene returned with Brick's manhattan, studying his beet-red face as he approached. He added some extra "pity" cherries to the drink, then smiled and walked away.

Brick cleared his throat, took a sip of water, and reached for his drink.

"All right, I admit it, the straight stuff isn't my strong suit. Manhattans are the closest I come to drinking like Don Draper."

"So, why not have your usual?"

Brick took a sip of the manhattan and again looked toward the door.

"Honestly? It's a little liquid courage before a blind date."

She set her elbow on the counter and rested her chin in the palm of her hand.

"Really?" she asked suggestively. "I wouldn't think you'd have any problems getting dates."

He took another sip, feeling a pleasant warmth soothing his irritated throat.

"My best friend's been trying to set me up with this girl for a while now, but I've never been big on fix-ups."

"No?" She seemed amused. "What do you know about her?"

"She sounds perfectly nice, works for the *Seattle P.I.* writing movie reviews. I guess she's around my age. Been single for a little while. That's about the sum of my knowledge."

"Ever seen a picture of her?"

"Nope."

"So, you have no idea what she looks like?"

Ransom shook his head. "Not a clue."

"And when is she supposed to get here?"

He gulped down another mouthful of alcohol and ice and looked at the clock.

"Any minute now."

His neighbor reached her hand over and set it on his forearm. "Do you want to get out of it? Maybe sneak off with me before then."

Hell yes!

Brick crunched the ice in his teeth.

"I'm sorry, but I don't think I could do that."

"Good answer," she replied as she nodded toward the front counter, "I think our table is ready."

Brick sat up straight, shaking his head to knock the thoughts into place. He looked toward the front desk, where the hostess was nodding to his drinking companion as she started in their direction, carrying two menus. She made a beeline for the Dalwhinnie-drinking mystery lady.

"Ms. Price, your table is ready."

"Thank you," Julie replied as she looked in Brick's direction. "Could you have the drinks added to our bill?"

"Of course," the hostess replied as she led the way toward the back of the restaurant.

Brick stood up, still feeling a little disoriented. Julie pointed to his glass before she turned and followed the hostess.

"Don't forget your drink."

He nodded dumbly as he grabbed the remainder of his manhattan and followed behind.

The hostess led them across the restaurant to one of the booths perpendicular to the windows facing 4th Avenue. She waited until they had taken their seats, then she set their menus in front of them, promised their server would be over in a moment, and left.

Brick heard nothing but the reverberating confusion in his head.

He sat on his side of the table, staring at the woman across from him.

This was Julie Price? Flynn had outdone himself!

Julie brushed her hair back behind her ears as she looked over the drink menu with those eyes of hers. Then she set it down and looked up at Brick with a bemused smile on her face.

"Nice to finally meet you Brick."

"Nice to meet *you*."

"Unlike you, I asked Flynn to show me a picture."

"Wish I'd done the same," he replied, searching for the words. "I hope that wasn't a turn-off back there…"

"What are you talking about? I think I lured you in nicely. Kind of fun having the upper hand for a change."

"I really didn't know what to expect. All I knew was you were some movie critic who my friend was helping find a date."

"So, you were thinking I was some sort of female film geek?"

"Yeah."

"And what exactly do 'female film geeks' look like?"

"Male film geeks," he replied immediately.

Julie laughed.

Maybe this would work out after all!

"I'm really not sure what I was expecting," Brick began. "All I know is that Flynn's wife, Morgan, love her as I may, has tried to set me up with a few...*unusual* women over the years."

"Such as?"

"Reliving it would be too painful, believe me. But just let me get one question out of the way up front. You do like movies, correct?"

"Very much. And you're a cop?" she asked in turn.

Brick smiled. "That I am."

"So, a film geek, that means you were expecting what? Like one of those *Ain't It Cool News* guys in the Utilikilts, minus the Adam's apple?"

"Exactly."

"I hate Utilikilts," Julie promised.

"Nasty, nasty things."

"Hope you aren't disappointed."

"Not one bit." Brick said with a grin.

"Listen, we can play twenty questions later," Julie interjected as she set her glass down and reached for the menu. "What looks good?"

~

As far as successful dates went, this was one for the record books. Not because of one thing in particular, but because of many things, that mysterious blend that ignites when there's just the right spark.

They made their way through the usual questionnaire, covering the gamut of work, family, and personal predilections. The results proved more than encouraging.

There was a reasonable degree of overlap in their literary and cultural interests, though Brick's taste in reading material obviously leaned heavily in the direction of cookbooks (peripheral reading in his current investigation not withstanding). As for Julie, not only did she like good food, but she knew more about wine than Brick could hope to absorb in a lifetime. The fact that she was beautiful and funny as hell? That just made things that much more fun.

Why hadn't Flynn introduced them sooner?

"How was it" Julie asked as Brick set his fork down for the last time.

"Perfect."

She reached across the table and sampled his crab cakes. Brick had already bartered several bites of her duck.

"I think yours was the best," she said. "Now what about dessert?"

"I'm impressed, a woman who actually goes for dessert."

"I'm not some Bellevue blond, Brick. When I go to dinner, I want to *eat.*"

He was falling in love.

"The waiter said something about tiramisu," Brick said.

"Blech, too creamy."

"I'm not a fan either. I'm going for either the coconut pie or the homemade donuts."

Julie set down her menu and motioned to the waiter.

"We'll have the pie and the donuts," she said. She looked at Ransom. "Espresso?"

He nodded.

"And two espressos."

"I'll have those right up," the waiter said as he took the menus and slipped away.

"We can share," Julie said. "I hope you're okay with me ordering."

"I admire a woman who takes control."

Julie Price fixed him in her gaze.

"You haven't seen *anything* yet."

Mochy's Mexican Cantina sat on a side street a couple blocks over from Old Town Ballard. It was the kind of place that made even its owner a little nervous about touching any of the surfaces before he ate, but the food was so damn good that none of the customers seemed to care. While most of the folks who went there were regulars, no one at the counter ever let on that they recognized them. Mochy's wasn't the kind of place for people who wanted to get chatty with the cooks or the diners at neighboring tables; it was for people who liked well-made, traditional Mexican food, along with their privacy, and everything about the place was fashioned with a focus on the meals and little else. Although the staff running the place knew the repeat customers' orders and drinks of choice by heart, they simply nodded their heads as they jotted down orders for meals that had often been put on the grill the moment the cook saw a particular individual walk in the door.

The front of the building hadn't been painted in decades, and the dilapidated exterior, where exposed, rotted wood siding peeked out from under blistered paint, sat in stark contrast to the newly constructed condos that towered just a few blocks north. A faded sandwich board, emblazoned with a drunken, sombrero-wearing Mochy Moose, sat by the curb, where it had resided undisturbed since it had been placed there on the restaurant's opening day several presidencies ago. Tonight, Mochy's peeling and faded expression of margarita-fueled bliss was quickly disappearing under the increasingly heavy snowfall. The cartoon liquor bubbles that floated around his antlers were completely engulfed in shadow as a figure in a dark trench coat approached the restaurant from the south and slipped in the front entrance.

Peter Cornelius was sitting in his usual spot, the darkest booth in the farthest corner of the back dining room. Like most of the folks eating there on this snowy night, the rotund man was a neighborhood regular, who usually arrived late, after the rush of mid-evening diners had departed. He always took the same high-backed booth, and he always sat on the same side, with his back to the entrance, which was covered with a frayed and worn beaded curtain that did its threadbare-best to block out whatever neon-tinged light attempted to seep into the nearly forgotten back reaches of the dive restaurant.

Tonight, like most nights, Cornelius was hunched over a detective book, an advanced copy of a title that would be coming out in a few months. Unlike most nights, he was actually enjoying what he was reading, and he kept his nose buried in the pages as he reached over with a deep-fried tortilla chip and scooped up a heavy portion of Mochy's fresh-made guacamole, which he carelessly shoved down his gullet, indifferent to the oily green chunks accumulating at the corners of his mouth.

The curtain rattled behind him and he heard footsteps approaching. A moment later a waitress appeared to his right and set down an enormous plate of rice and beans, along with a covered container filled with steaming tortillas, and a plate overflowing with charred onions, peppers, and grilled steak strips, and topped with a glistening, serrated steak knife. Cornelius didn't look up to thank her, but merely shoved aside the empty guacamole dish along with his drained margarita glass.

"Gimme another Cadillac," he grunted.

The waitress picked up the empty glass and left without

saying a word.

Cornelius turned the page and continued reading. He reached for the steak knife, sawed off a chunk of meat, and lifted the lid on the container of tortillas. The steam from the container rose in the cool air and fogged the lenses on his round eyeglasses. He tore off a portion of tortilla, slathered it with sour cream and salsa, stuffed it with pepper, cheese, and the piece of steak, and shoved it in his mouth before the fog had cleared from his glasses.

The beaded curtain clattered behind him and footsteps approached to his side as he set the steak knife back on the plate.

"Where's that margarita?" Cornelius demanded as he smacked his gummy lips and continued reading.

A shadow stepped in from the side, and a torn page of newsprint was thrown down on top of his plate. Cornelius looked over in alarm. It was an advanced copy of a review that would be running that weekend, his cover piece on Daniel Buckley's latest. The headline read: *Hack Fiction*.

Cornelius' eyes moved from the paper to the figure standing over him; they narrowed when he made the connection.

"What the hell does it matter to you?"

He got no response. The shadow hovered over him a moment longer. Then it moved toward him suddenly. Light glinted off the edge of the steak knife, briefly flashing across Cornelius' eyes in the half-second before one gloved hand covered his mouth, and the other seized the worn handle and swept the serrated blade toward his throat. Cornelius tried to yell for help, but his voice was cut to a gurgle as he fought to free himself from the booth. His hands swept across the table, trying like hell to reach for the plates, to sweep the platters and bowl onto the floor. He let out one last garbled cry as the serrated blade tore into his throat and sawed through his neck. As quickly and violently as it began, it was done. The heavy figure fell lifelessly to the surface of the table, his face and head turned at an impossible angle atop the platter of peppers and steak. Hot, dark blood burbled from his neck, pooling on the table and dripping from the edge, as Cornelius' attacker grabbed the knife and slipped out the back door.

A moment later, the waitress passed through the beaded curtain, carrying a large margarita. She walked through the darkness of the back room and approached Peter Cornelius' booth, where his body lay slumped across his final meal. Before she could make out what had happened, her foot slipped in the pooling blood on the floor. She fell to one knee and found herself staring into Cornelius' bulging, lifeless eyes. A wad of newspaper was shoved in his mouth, and she could just make out where the other blood-soaked end emerged from his slashed throat. She threw the drink to the ground and screamed.

*   *   *

The drive back to Greenwood had taken significantly longer than usual. The snow wasn't making getting around the city any easier. Plus, Brick hadn't wanted to take any chances driving home with booze in his system. He and Julie had stayed at the Dahlia so long that the hostess had eventually come over and let them know that a another party was waiting for their table, so they'd slipped across the street to Lola to grab some coffee and continue talking.

Brick talked about police work and cooking. Julie

talked about writing and movies. And they had continued to pinpoint the areas in which their interests met. Most importantly, something clicked. Clicked in a way Brick wasn't used to. That was a very good sign.

Since Julie lived nearby in Belltown, that had given him a chance to walk her back to her apartment, where one thing led to another and he'd wound up giving her one hell of a good night kiss in the lobby of her building. Only, come to think of it, maybe *she* had kissed *him*. Either way, that had been it, and it had been more than enough. For now.

Only that wasn't it. Not entirely anyway. On the walk back to his car, the gears had started turning. He liked this woman. A *lot*. And for the first time in he couldn't remember how long, his imagination was starting to get the better of him.

The first sign of trouble came when he got home and started pondering breakfast. Not that he was hungry, but he felt he had to think optimistically if he wanted the best-case scenario to play out. And as far as Brick was concerned, the best-case scenario was to take Julie out again, and maybe next time he'd be making her breakfast the following morning.

The second sign of trouble came when Flynn called his phone and Brick actually answered. If the date had gone badly he'd have done his best to dodge the call. If the date had been a one-off run around the bases, he'd have been "away from his phone." The fact that he was home and eager to run the play-by-play meant Brick was in bigger trouble than he thought.

"It went really well, man," Brick said as he set a pan on the stove, turned the dial to 5, and set a carton of eggs on the counter.

"What's that noise?" Flynn asked.

"Oh, I'm making an omelette."

"Didn't you just eat?"

"Yeah, but with the way things went, I expect to be fixing her breakfast soon enough."

"Since when are you such an optimist?" Flynn asked. "You really must have liked her."

"Why didn't you set me up with her sooner?"

"I tried!"

"Well, you should have tried harder."

"Anyway, I'm glad it went well." Flynn replied. "Now, do you mind if I give you a word of advice?"

Brick felt a pre-emptive surge of annoyance as he grabbed the Pam and sprayed the pan.

"What?"

"You might not want to actually *eat* what you cook."

"What the hell does that mean?"

"I'm just saying, something like that this late probably isn't gonna burn off. I think we're reaching a sort of metabolic turning point at our age and-"

"What are you saying, I'm gaining weight?"

"Well…"

"Thanks a whole hell of a lot, man!"

He switched the phone to his shoulder as he sliced off a chunk of onion, diced it carefully, and scraped the pieces into the pan to sauté. He rinsed the sharp blade under the faucet and wiped it dry on a towel. Though he liked to discuss cooking, Brick was loath to mention his knife skills, which were adequate, but hampered by a fairly severe fear of knives. Not a helpful attribute for an aspiring chef.

Flynn just laughed. "Listen, just make sure you aren't

counting your chickens before they're hatched, OK?"

Ransom picked up an egg, thonked it on the counter, and cracked it into the pan, where it sizzled and danced over the greased surface.

"You know the saying, Flynn," Brick said as he reached for a second egg, which he also thwacked on the counter and started to crack open. "You've gotta break some eggs if you wanna" -- a bloody egg fell into the pan -- *"Shit."*

Brick stared down in revulsion.

"I don't think that's how the phrase goes-" Flynn said after a moment of silence.

The phone beeped and a second call came in. Brick, still grimacing, looked from the horror-movie omelette to the caller ID. It was O'Brien.

"Hold on. I think I've got to take this."

*   *   *

"So much for a slow start on the job," Brick said.

He was standing in the middle of the restaurant's back room. The smell of grease hung heavy in the air, along with the aroma of Folgers coffee, which the cook had handed out to several of the cops on the scene. Brick had taken a pass; so far as he was concerned Folgers wasn't coffee, but it seemed every other cop on the scene had accepted the offer of bottom-shelf caffeine, as everyone around him was carrying a diner mug full of the stuff. The sour, stale stench was making him almost as sick to his stomach as the bloody crime scene was.

The hulking body was still slumped over the table. A wide circle of blood had pooled around the booth, making it difficult for anyone to approach without getting it on their shoes. Brick leaned in from the side of the booth, doing his best to avoid the drying, sticky mess. Making things even gorier, it appeared the victim had put up a respectable fight, probably punching and flailing even after the knife had made its first fatal pass through his carotid artery before sawing its way through his windpipe, cutting the thick tissue like a crunchy, sunbaked garden hose.

"Who is this guy?" Ransom asked O'Brien, who had shown up in a very '70s looking tracksuit, with triple stripes running up each leg and arm. "Nice outfit, by the way."

"Thank you," O'Brien replied. "Victim is Peter Cornelius. 47. He's the book reviewer for *The Seattle Times*. Owners say he was a regular. Lived in the Canal Station Condos up the street."

"Book critic, eh?"

"I know. I know. I can already see where your mind is going."

Brick scratched his chin sleepily as he surveyed the gory scene.

"And this went down while people were in here *eating*?"

"Sort of. Happened close to 10:30 when the place was pretty quiet. Restaurant is open late. Usually has a big dinner rush, followed by a quiet stretch from 9:30 to 1 a.m. when the bars start letting out and folks come over here for late night grub to soak up the booze. 'Bout the time this happened, the only other customers were a few bar-hoppers at the front counter who had stopped in for tacos. The owner says Cornelius came in around 10. I guess that was pretty typical for him. Didn't like crowds. Always sat in this same booth, liked to be left alone while he ate. Waitress came in with his meal around 10:20, left to make him another drink, came back a few minutes later and found him like this."

"I don't suppose this restaurant has any security cameras."

"Place is barely standing. You think they're gonna spend money on security cameras?"

"Never hurts to ask. And *nobody* saw the killer come in?"

O'Brien shook his head. "Like I say, waitress was doing double duty making the drinks. The owner was in the back. The cook saw someone walking in out of the corner of his eye, but he didn't think anything of it."

"And there was no one at the counter who saw this person or recognized them from the neighborhood?"

O'Brien shook his head. "No one has come forward yet."

"The cook, did he say if it was a man or a woman at least?" Brick asked.

"Nope. But if you want my opinion, look at this booth," he motioned toward the table. "Dude had his throat cut with a serrated steak knife. That's what they figure he used. The knife from his plate of fajitas. Now look at this-" O'Brien reached over and picked a knife up from a nearby table. He held it where Brick could get a close look at the dull, almost rounded teeth on the blade. "They don't exactly keep the knives here razor sharp. Plus, we're dealing with a big guy who was fighting for his life while someone used one of these things to saw through his throat. The killer had to have some *serious* upper body strength, which indicates it was most likely a man."

A photographer was taking pictures of the room from the back corner. The flash reflected off of a plastic evidence bag that was sitting on the bench opposite the body. A blood-soaked sheet of newsprint was sealed inside.

"What's in the bag?" Brick asked.

"You're gonna *love* that," a voice behind him murmured.

Brick turned to see Anne Sullivan walking through the beaded curtain carrying two Starbucks cups. She handed him one.

"There's a 24-hour place down the street. Somehow I knew I wouldn't be the only one passing on the house blend here," she said. "Sorry, they didn't have any cinnamon rolls."

"Thank you,' Brick said. "If only you weren't married."

Anne stepped toward the table, her foot landing squarely in the middle of the congealing blood puddle as she reached over and grabbed the plastic bag from the bench. Her shoe made a sticky suction sound as she stepped back and turned to Ransom and O'Brien so they could see the bag.

"Advanced copy of *The Times*' weekend book review," she said. "Mr. Cornelius here wrote the cover piece."

Brick stared at the bloody newspaper.

"Is that a review of Dan Buckley's latest book?"

Anne nodded. "Yep, a pretty thorough evisceration, too."

"And where did you find it?"

O'Brien motioned toward the booth. "Stuffed down the reviewer's windpipe," O'Brien replied.

Brick brought his hand up to his throat as he imagined the sequence in which the scene must have played out. His eyes darted back and forth across the booth, picturing the movements of Cornelius and his attacker. He could see the killer stepping forward, grabbing the knife from the plate, and sweeping it up to the critic's neck. The struggle, the awkward shape of the knife handle twisting in the killer's hand. He could almost *hear* the tearing, sawing sounds the blade must have made as it sliced through the tendons and tissue of the throat. Then his eyes settled on the opposite corner of the booth, specifically on a section of wood above the seat cushions, where he noticed what appeared to be a smeared, bloody handprint.

"Anne, I sure as hell hope that isn't the work of one of your guys," Brick said as he motioned toward the handprint.

Anne leaned in and studied it closely. "I'm positive it isn't."

"Think there's any chance of getting a print?"

"Attacker was most likely wearing gloves, but who knows, maybe they slipped off in the struggle. Good case, we get a print. Best case, the killer got cut in the struggle and we get some DNA."

"You think no knife means it broke on him?" Brick asked.

"Who knows. That or maybe he didn't think to drop it till he'd walked out of here," Anne replied.

Brick motioned toward the back door. "Lets get some of the guys to sweep the dumpsters, the back alley, and any nearby lots to see if the killer chucked it on his way out of here."

"Absolutely," Anne said with a nod.

Brick turned back to O'Brien.

"You said Cornelius lived up the street?"

"That's what they tell me."

"We might as well head on up there then."

~

The sun was just peeking over the horizon when they finally got the go-ahead to search Cornelius' condo, but it took a couple more hours to track down the building's property manager, show him the search warrant, and convince him to hand over a copy of the keys to the deceased

book critic's unit. By the time Ransom and O'Brien pushed
the door open and began to look around, the Ballard streets
outside were coming to life with morning activity. Traffic was
rumbling past the building, and they could hear pedestrians
and their canine companions bustling by on the sidewalks
one story down.

It was a one-bedroom unit with a wide-open living room
and kitchen, and an office space set up in a side room in the
south corner. Every wall in the entryway, the living room, the
den, and the hallway leading back to the master bedroom was
covered with book-lined wooden shelves. Books were piled
in meticulously-arranged stacks wherever there was a square
foot of space: atop end tables, chairs, footstools, Brick even
caught sight of a few hardbacks lined up along the top of
the toilet tank in the bathroom. The very thought of which
triggered his most deep-seated Howard Hughes-like phobias.
Then, like sediment that had washed in to fill the cracks
between the larger glacial deposits, there were newspapers,
journals, and printed sheets of papers neatly piled, filed, and
folded into and among all of the paperbacks, hardcovers, and
galley copies that comprised the floor-to-ceiling collection of
printed materials.

"This man must have had ink running through his
veins," O'Brien observed as he crossed the room and picked a
stack of papers up from the coffee table. He flipped through
the pages and looked at Ransom. "These are all printed
emails. He must have read everything in hard copy."

"So *this* is the guy that *'think before you print this'* email
stamp was written for!"

Brick walked past his partner as he made a beeline for the
office. The air inside was thick with the smell of aging paper,

but the surfaces were all remarkably dust free.

"He must have a cleaning lady," Brick observed. "No way a bachelor could keep things this neat." He knew that first-hand.

"That would make sense," O'Brien said as he took a seat on the couch and continued flipping through the stack of pages.

Brick shuffled through the papers on the desk, most of which appeared to be printed emails as well. He sorted through them quickly. A name in one of the subject lines immediately caught his eye. *Daniel Buckley.*

The subject lines for several of the emails read: *Re: Daniel Buckley review backlash*, and *Re: Daniel Buckley inquiry.* All had been sent by a D. Barrow with a Comcast email account.

Well. Well. What do we have here?

Brick pulled out the desk chair and took a seat.

The chair creaked and shifted under him; apparently, the weight of the sedentary book reviewer had thoroughly broken it down over the years. It felt as though all of the cushioning had been compacted into a thin layer of pulverized dust. Brick settled in the chair and began to read a few of the emails. The second message caught his eye. He'd read a portion of it somewhere before. After the introductory first paragraph, the text was indented and placed in italics, where it read:

"Hackneyed writing, ridiculous story."

And a few lines down:

"Trite characters, absurd plot, action that is simply beyond the pale. If you have time to kill in a waiting room before a colonoscopy, as I did, then I suppose there are worse books out there."

This was one of the Amazon reviews he'd skimmed over the other morning. Only, the introduction to the letter indicated the person who had posted this particular review had wound up receiving a string of threatening emails and taunting messages on Facebook and Twitter. It didn't give the reviewer's name.

Brick cleared his throat as he pondered his own reaction to the negative review when he'd looked it over the day before.

The next email was also from Barrow, but was sent in regard to a different individual. It, too, detailed what seemed to be a similar pattern. The person in question had merely posted a review of Daniel Buckley's latest book on their website, and mentioned it on a social media site, only to experience a barrage of nasty online contacts from an unidentified individual soon after.

"Hey, can you come take a look at this?"

O'Brien, who was sitting on the couch looking totally shell-shocked, lowered what he was reading and walked over, still holding the pages in his hand.

"What do you make of these?" Brick asked. "Both are about five months old."

O'Brien scanned them, then wordlessly handed Ransom what he'd been looking at himself.

It was a letter sent by someone also claiming to be David Barrow, who identified himself as the head of the Greenwood Mystery Writers Circle, a local genre-writing and hard-boiled fiction group. Two newspaper clippings, both of them from *The Seattle Times,* were stapled to the letter. Both articles detailed local homicides that had occurred four and five months earlier. Brick scanned the articles, then read the letters closely. The long and the short of Barrow's letter was clear: He suspected Daniel Buckley of being involved in the deaths of two of his acquaintances who had died under mysterious circumstances – thoroughly detailed in the news articles – but he had gotten the brush-off from the Seattle Police and thought he'd take the story to the media to get it some exposure.

"You remember hearing anything about this?" Brick asked.

"It's always possible, but there's been nothing that I can recall."

"Assuming the dates on these emails are legit, and they both came from the author of that letter, there might be a link between all of these cases."

O'Brien reached for the letter and news clippings again. As he drew his arm back, his tracksuit sleeve brushed against the mouse, waking Cornelius' computer from its sleep. A Word document flashed onto the screen, the cursor blinking hypnotically at the end of a half-written paragraph in the middle of the page. The headline read:

Did Bestselling Seattle Author Kill For 'Cheap Thrills?'

The piece was still in very rough shape, and if he had to guess, Brick would have said it could never have run as it was without inviting a massive lawsuit, but it did detail some fascinating if very conspiracy-heavy events.

"This cuts off before it gives us either of the victims' names, but it sure looks like they were going to be the same as the ones in those death notices," Ransom observed as he finished reading the half-written piece. He returned to the email printouts, tapping his index finger on the review excerpts. "Think Anne and her team can work with Amazon to determine when and where these reviews were posted?"

"I'm sure they've done it before."

"What do you think the chances are that the names of the victims in those news clippings will match the names of the folks who posted those reviews?"

"Wouldn't surprise me in the least," O'Brien mused.

"Either Dan Buckley has a dangerously thin skin, or he's got one hell of a rabid fan."

"Or someone wants us to think that anyway," O'Brien countered.

Brick took David Barrow's letter, grabbed a pencil from the desk, and jotted the return address down on a piece of paper, tearing off the corner as he got to his feet. He looked down at the paper again.

"Kind of a weird address. Where do you suppose that is exactly, Fremont?"

O'Brien studied the street numbers. "Ever seen that '70s John Wayne cop movie 'McQ?'"

"No. It any good?"

"It's flat-out terrible, but 'McQ' lived on a boat beneath the Aurora Bridge. I'm pretty sure that's in the same vicinity."

Brick nodded as he mentally mapped it out. That would put Barrow's place right on the water between Fremont and Gas Works Park on the north shore of Lake Union.

"Can you finish things up and get Anne and her boys in here to scour this place?" Brick asked.

"Sure," O'Brien said as he stood and followed Ransom into the living room. "But I'm warning you, next case *I'm* going to be the one running off to do all the fun stuff, and I'll be leaving *you* to deal with the humdrum logistical matters."

"Fair enough," Ransom replied.

No way he would let that happen.

"You going to talk to Barrow?"

"I'm gonna try," Brick said as he headed for the door. "Oh, one last thing. Can you confirm that Daniel Buckley definitely doesn't have a Washington State driver's license, and that he's *never* had one here or anywhere else in the country?"

O'Brien looked confused. "Sure," he said as his eyebrows pinched together.

*   *   *

Brick took a right at the Fremont Troll -- a massive concrete sculpture of a, well, troll, that sat hunkered under the Aurora Bridge, forever smashing a classic Volkswagen bug into smithereens -- and rode the brake down the length of Troll Avenue, the steep two-lane street that ran directly beneath the bridge. Fortunately, the road conditions had improved a bit as the overnight ice and snow continued to melt away with the rising daytime temperatures. He took a left at the bottom of the hill and wound around till the numbers started to echo Barrow's address. Sure enough, he eventually found himself parked in the lot for a marina.

Ransom climbed out of the car and headed toward a metal security gate situated at the top of a metal ramp leading down to a network of floating docks. He looked over the list of names posted behind a Plexiglass cover to the side of the door. In the middle of the bunch he saw:

Barrow, D – #37.

Easy enough so far.

Getting through the security gate was no problem either, seeing as someone had been thoughtful enough to jam it open with what appeared to be a rock-hard Krispy Kreme doughnut. Brick slipped through the rusty gate, studying the petrified breakfast treat as he passed. He'd be sure to remember *that* the next time he drove past the shop and was tempted by the lure of the "Hot Donuts" sign.

The marina was sleepy this early in the morning, but a few boaters were scattered on the decks here and there, staining wood railings and scrubbing various fiberglass surfaces. Brick nodded at the people who smiled at him, and muttered a few bits of snidery under his breath to the one or two particularly crusty codgers who gave him the stink eye when they saw him. As he passed an ancient tugboat, which might have been rather cool were it not for the large swaths of rust and duct tape that comprised roughly 75 percent of the vessel's shell, Brick noticed a young man of medium height, clad in workout pants and a gray tank top, who was doing chin-ups on a metal contraption that had been bolted to the one section of the boat that was apparently still structurally sound. A lit cigarette was clenched in the guy's front teeth, and he took a long drag at the bottom of each chin-up.

Brick nodded hello and received a terse nod in return.

Interesting crowd.

The next spot over was #37, which, it turned out, was the berth of an enormous, immaculately maintained white sailboat. The name on the back of the ship read: *Highland Hangover.*

A guy in his late 30s, with dark, slicked-back hair, was seated in a chair on deck. He was wearing jeans and a heavy sweatshirt with a drawing of an egg standing on end. Under the egg was the caption *"Make Mine Hard-Boiled."* The silhouette of a handgun was silk-screened below the words.

He was reading a hardback copy of *The Big Sleep*. Dude was apparently a huge hard-boiled mystery nerd.

This had to be David Barrow.

Brick stopped at the railing and waited to be noticed. When Barrow failed to see him, Brick cleared his throat just a hair louder than was absolutely necessary.

Barrow looked up from his book. "Can I help you with something?"

"I hope so," Brick replied. He pulled his wallet from his pocket and flashed his badge. "I'm Detective Ransom with the Seattle Police Department."

Barrow lowered his book, his face falling slightly. "What's this about?"

"Nothing to be worried about," Brick said. "You're not in trouble, Mr. Barrow. It *is* Mr. Barrow, correct?"

Barrow nodded, his eyebrows pulling together as his apprehension grew by the second. "What's this about?" he asked again.

"I have some questions related to a series of messages you exchanged with a Mr. Peter Cornelius from *The Seattle Times* over the last several months."

Barrow stood quickly. "Oh, yes." He walked over and reached out his free hand to help Brick climb aboard. "Did he finally convince you guys to open a case?"

"Well, in a way he may have."

Barrow looked back at him blankly.

Ransom found his footing and watched Barrow's face, looking for tells.

"I'm afraid Mr. Cornelius is dead."

"Dead?"

"He was murdered."

Barrow locked eyes with him. "It was Buckley, wasn't it?"

"Why do you say that?"

Barrow pointed to a folded newspaper that was lying on the deck beside his chair. "You mean besides that review in this morning's paper? The same reasons I've been giving Peter for months. Dan Buckley is the one person I can think of who could have known *both* Theresa and Sarah and had a grudge with them - the guy is notorious for taking criticism badly. I'm pretty sure Cornelius was starting to think the same thing. Now he's dead too?"

"Well, frankly, we're not sure what Cornelius thought, not yet anyway, but yes, the fact that we're here shows he was probably giving your theory some credence. He was working on something that raised the same questions for us. Now these victims you mention-"

"Theresa Carpenter and Sarah Beers."

"Theresa and Sarah," Brick repeated. "Who were they?"

"Two members of the Greenwood Mystery Writers Circle."

"And how did they know Dan Buckley?"

"They met him at one of our meetings a few years back, before he'd really broken into the big time."

"And what was he doing at your meeting?"

"His publisher, Catacomb Press, used to send some of their new authors to talk to the group from time to time. They thought we might be able to start a little grassroots word of mouth if we liked what we heard. Buckley and some younger guy came to one of our meetings at Neptune Coffee. Wheeled in a couple boxes of *On The Money*, held a little reading, then hung out for a while as we went over our own stuff."

"And did you like what you read of the book? Were you guys fans of Buckley's work?"

"It was OK. Certainly had a clear voice and a lot of promise," Barrow said as he held up the book he'd been reading. "I mean, Daniel Buckley is no Chandler, but he's not bad. Personally, I share the opinion of a lot of hard-boiled detective fans. I'd prefer it if he stuck to his current writing style but worked on some grittier plots, like the ones in his earlier books. Unfortunately, I think his publisher is afraid a return to really bloody pulp mysteries might knock him back out of the mainstream."

Brick nodded. This was the second time he'd heard something less than idolatrous about Dan Buckley's current fiction, but niche fanatics claiming writers or entertainers had lost their edge just when the rest of the world became aware of them wasn't something new. Flynn had been lamenting *Metallica's* "selling out" since their high school days.

"Forgive me for cutting to the chase here, but I have to tell you, I've met Dan Buckley, and the man doesn't strike me as a threatening type. From everything I've heard, he takes jabs rather gracefully. Is there something more you're basing this on?"

"I don't mean how he acts in public appearances. I'm talking about how he acts when someone criticizes his work outside of the media spotlight. Did you see the review links I sent Cornelius for Buckley's last book?"

"The negative ones?"

Barrow nodded.

"Yeah, I've seen quite a few the last few days. Cornelius had a bunch of them printed out."

"Theresa and Sarah published two of the most critical

reactions, and both of them started getting harassing phone calls and email messages shortly afterwards. Your typical readers and Amazon customers wouldn't have known how to reach them. Same thing happened with a few other folks that ran stuff online. Nasty comments popped up in the response sections, bunch of personal attack campaigns cropped up on whatever social media sites they used."

"And you think Buckley was behind those?"

"I do. Some of them at least."

"Doesn't that seem a bit... thin though? Jumping from a few bad reviews to murder? The Internet is full of comments from cranks and cockmonkeys; why would these two girls, who, no offense, were mostly unknown, get that much attention for posting a couple of reviews that panned his book?"

"Writers are a vengeful lot, detective. Ever pissed one off? If they don't fly off the handle to your face, they're still inclined to write you into one of their books, usually as a corpse."

Brick crossed his arms, trying his damnedest to keep his expression even, but he could feel his head cocking at an angle and one corner of his mouth pulling back to his ear in a skeptical half-smirk.

"OK then," Barrow elaborated, "what if I told you Buckley and his friend from Catacomb went to the Pig n Whistle after the meeting with a few of the women from our group?"

"That might raise a few red flags. It at least shows a clear connection. Do you recall who was there specifically?"

"Theresa and Sarah were two of them, of course. The others I don't remember. "

"Any idea if anything happened when they went out?"

"Not that I know of. I think one of them might have seen Buckley's friend a couple more times after that-"

"The Catacomb employee. Any idea who that was?"

"I'd never seen him before, but his name was something short, like a videogame character-"

"Something like 'Zack?'"

Barrow's eyes narrowed. "Quite possibly. Lemme ask you something else. You on the D.J. Norman case too?"

"You're up on your news."

"The Seattle mystery community is a tight-knit group. I downloaded a podcast from the *Slash and Grab* talk last weekend and heard how she laid into Buckley. I don't think her comments were fair, but now *she's* dead too? I mean, come on, if Buckley isn't somehow involved in both cases, then someone is trying their damnedest to set him up. He acted like a gentleman at that appearance, but like I said, he knew that was being recorded, and there were TV and newspaper reporters there all weekend. Once the recorders and cameras were gone, I'd be willing to bet he let her have it one way or the other."

"OK, I'm gonna look into this a little more. Is there anyone else in your group that I should talk to?"

"It actually disbanded a couple months ago, folks stopped showing up for meetings after Theresa and Sarah's...you know. But I can send out an email and ask people to get in touch with you if they have some information."

"That would be good."

"Oh, and if you're interested in seeing how Daniel Buckley *really* deals with his readers, you might try going to his reading at Elliot Bay Books tonight. If he lets them do a

Q and A, it usually gets…interesting."

Suddenly, the chin-up guy on the neighboring boat started catcalling.

"*Helloooooooo,*" The guy called over.

Brick turned his head to see what was happening. Apparently, after his workout, the tugboat owner liked to sip on a Rainier and stir up trouble. He took a big sip from his can of beer, then shouted over again.

"Hey, Barrow! Why don't you stop chewing that guy's ear off and get yourself a *real* boat?!"

"Out of curiosity, what kind of boat is this?" Brick asked.

"It's a 50-foot Beneteau Sense-" Barrow began-

He was interrupted by a howling sound, as his neighbor started running around on the deck of the tugboat, screaming, "Why don't you sail to *Dooblin?! Doooblin*, England!"

"Suck it, Golding!" Barrow screamed back.

"Nice little community you have here," Brick observed.

"He's just mad because I cleaned him out at poker last night," Barrow said. Then he raised his voice so his neighbor could hear. "If that dinghy of his wasn't taking on water I'd have taken *that* too*!*"

Brick looked from Barrow to Golding and back again. He took out a business card, which he handed over like a ticket to leave.

"Clearly this is a bad time. If you happen to get ahold of anyone from your group that might have anything useful to add, tell them to give me a call. I'm going to take your advice and check out that reading tonight."

"Good. Trust me, just see what he's like if someone gets under his skin. It's practically guaran-"

He was cut off by a flurry of turkey sounds that warbled in from the tugboat nearby. Barrow waited till it seemed the exercising interloper was tired out before he continued.

"I think you just might see things from a similar vantage point if you catch Dan Buckley with his guard down."

"Maybe I will," Brick replied just before he climbed back down to the boardwalk and headed up the ramp toward the parking lot.

In fact, he most definitely would.

*   *   *

As luck would have it, by the time Ransom had found parking up the street and hoofed it down the hill to the Elliott Bay Book Company, Daniel Buckley had finished his reading and was more than halfway through a question-and-answer session with the members of the audience, who were packed into the rows of moveable auditorium chairs like eggs in a carton.

Brick walked past the front counter, where a number of the store's staff members were ringing up customers while their coworkers stood and watched the event taking place at the other end of the massive store space. A sign by the register showed the image of a cell phone with a red slash through it. The text beneath the picture asked people to switch off their phones during author readings. Brick snatched his handset from his pocket and powered it down. He knew the sting of Seattle's anti-cell-phone sneer all too well, and he sure as hell didn't want to be on the receiving end of it again! He continued past the table of new and noteworthy books that occupied the front of the store, and took a position beside a shelf of graphic novels toward the back of the event space.

Elliott Bay was one of Seattle's oldest bookstores. It had

originally been located in a labyrinthine old brick building in Pioneer square, which had given the store a seemingly limitless number of nooks and crannies in which to place pine shelves full of books and journals, all spread out over a landscape of creaking, wide-planked wooden floors. As Pioneer Square fell onto hard times after the financial crisis, the store's owner had finally decided to pull up stakes and relocate the business to a large industrial space up the hill in the Capitol Hill neighborhood, where it had been open ever since. The new space had most of the same shelves and fixtures, but little in the way of nooks and crannies, and Ransom felt it had never recaptured the same magic as the original space. Yet the one thing it most definitely *did* have in common with the original store were the creaking wood floors, a fact he was painfully aware of as he tried his best to silently make his way to the back of the standing-room-only crowd.

So far, it didn't appear Buckley had lost his cool or gone off on the crowd as David Barrow seemed to feel was an inevitable turn of events at any Daniel Buckley event. If anything, Buckley seemed to have the crowd eating from the palm of his hand as the assortment of middle-aged readers and senior citizens laughed along knowingly and graciously each time the author delivered a supposedly off-the-cuff but clearly well-rehearsed anecdote.

Then a college-aged girl in the front row raised her hand. Buckley's mouth cracked into a big smile when he nodded in her direction, and he continued watching her closely as she walked up to the front of the stage and accepted the microphone from the event hostess.

Then she delivered her question.

"Mr. Buckley, thank you again for coming tonight. My question is for your older fans, who might prefer the flavor of your first few books. Do you have any reassuring words for readers who miss the raw feel of your early works?"

Buckley's grin was long gone by the time the question had drawn to a close. He locked her in place with a withering gaze.

"Phew..." Buckley said with a tone of forced dismissiveness. "I guess I'd just say to buy the latest edition of my first book, *On The Money,* and continue rereading it, ad nauseam, till an updated edition gets released, then switch them out and start all over again."

The audience tittered nervously.

"Is uh, is that a serious answer?" The girl asked.

"Is that a serious *question?*" Buckley countered. "Look, do me a favor, if you don't like my writing, or you don't like the way my books have progressed, stop reading them. The general public seems to like what I'm doing. The last three titles have debuted at the top of the New York Times Bestseller list, but if you don't *personally* like where I'm going, then just find yourself another author. I don't need-" He caught himself. "I won't take it personally."

Brick glanced around the room. The audience sat stone-faced.

Well, that was one way to quiet a crowd.

The store's moderator walked over and took the microphone. She stepped up on stage and proceeded to throw Dan Buckley a few high and slow softball questions, which he politely and humorously smacked away using just enough charm to bring the audience to its feet and back to his side. After a few more questions and a promise to 'stick around until every book is signed,' Buckley trudged away from the lectern and the audience headed to the registers to ring up their copies of *Cheap Thrills* before they queued up in line to get them autographed.

Brick had brought the copy of the book that Maureen Alexander had given him, it was concealed in a manila evidence envelope under his arm as he watched the crowd.

He homed in on Buckley, observing his actions closely. The guy did have an edge to him, just like Barrow had said, but the girl asking the questions had also been undeniably rude.

Yet, it appeared Dan Buckley was quick to shrug off irritation. To watch him now, one would never have suspected he had engaged in such a testy public exchange just a few moments earlier. What's more, it didn't appear he had lost anyone in the crowd. The guy had an edge, but he clearly had charm as well.

Buckley took a sip from a bottle of water as he chatted with the store's event host. Then he turned and greeted a thin, impeccably dressed brunette woman who was clad in an extremely expensive-looking suit. She walked over and gave him a warm kiss on the lips. Buckley put his arm around her and pulled her close. Aside from a raffishly seductive streak of silver that started at her temple and shot back through her pulled-back hair, if Ransom had had to guess her age, he'd have put this woman at just under 35. Yet he knew for a fact that she was 41. That was no blind guess either; this lady was beautiful, and famous, and wealthy as all hell, not to mention the clearest example Brick could pinpoint to support the unpopular claim that money really *could* buy happiness. Just as Zack Baxter had insinuated, Dan Buckley was definitely mingling with the who's who of Seattle society these days.

It would be hard to top this one though. The woman Buckley had just kissed and was now holding tightly was Beverly Pepper, the younger sister of Seattle's own Jeff Pepper, global software company co-founder and multi-billionaire. Beverly was the head of the Pepper Family Foundation, a non-profit charitable behemoth in Seattle, which was slowly but surely expanding its sites to include national projects in every corner of the country. Her older brother had co-founded a company that had essentially given birth to the world's computing industry, which in turn resulted in a virtually unlimited influx of wealth that had eventually led to, if not demanded the creation of, a massive charitable organization to manage and distribute the money Jeff Pepper was unable to spend on mammoth yachts and impulsive multimillion dollar flights of fancy, like domestic space-tourism companies, research organizations, and international science fiction museums. The fact that Daniel Buckley had his hand on this woman's ass meant he had reached the big time. (That wasn't to say her ass was anything less than perfectly toned.)

Brick waited till the store's hostess had stepped away, then he headed toward the front of the crowd and got the author's attention.

"Detective Ransom," Buckley said as he eyed the evidence envelope under Ransom's arm. "What can I do for you?"

"Good evening," Ransom said as he took the envelope from under his arm and held it in the opposite hand. "I was talking to some local mystery fans today and they told me about this event. Thought I ought to come by."

"Well, I hope you enjoyed it," Buckley replied as he glanced at his date.

He clearly wanted this exchange to be over and done with as soon as possible, ideally without the uncomfortable need to introduce Brick to Beverly Pepper, as that would necessitate having to explain why exactly a Seattle homicide detective was talking to him in the first place.

Brick turned his attention to Buckley's date and put out his free hand. "Ms. Pepper, Brick Ransom, I admire the work you and your brother are doing."

Beverly Pepper shook his hand, even as she gave Buckley a *'who's this guy?'* look. "Thank you very much, I appreciate that," she said.

"I just wish you guys could do something about the way my computer loses its internet connection once a week," Brick continued.

Beverly flashed a pained smile at the threadbare wisecrack. "Well, you'd have to talk to my brother about that one."

"Detective Buckley is looking into the Diane Norman shooting," Buckley interjected as he again looked at the envelope.

"Oh, that was such a terrible thing!" Pepper exclaimed. "I really used to love her books. Do you have any leads yet?"

"At this point, anything is a possibility. I promise you, when I figure it out you'll be among the first to know. But I hate to discuss something as awful as all that at an event like this."

"Then you're here on your own, not as part of the investigation?" Buckley asked.

"Well, cases are always in the back of my mind, but yeah,

I came here primarily for my own amusement. I was also wondering if you might be able to sign something for me," Brick said as he raised the envelope and plunked it down on the table.

Brick watched Buckley's face as he slowly lifted the corner of the envelope and slid a copy of *Cheap Thrills* out onto the tabletop. Buckley's shoulders relaxed visibly.

"I hope you don't mind," Ransom explained, "but Maureen Alexander gave me a free copy when I met with her the other day."

"Of course I don't mind," Buckley said, his voice suddenly ten times lighter as he took the book, spun it around, and flipped the cover open. Brick watched his hands as he pulled the cap off a Sharpie and signed his name in the front. "After all, each book is just an advertisement for another copy. Are you enjoying it so far?"

"Quite a bit actually."

"Then you're not one of the increasing number of readers disappointed with where the series is going?"

"Not in the slightest," Ransom answered as he studied Buckley's hands.

No cuts, no bandages.

"Although, now that you mention old fans," Brick said, as if the topic had just popped into his mind. "I did come across some information about two early fans I think you might be familiar with."

"Oh?" Buckley looked up expectantly. "Are you going to tell me who they are or keep me in suspense?"

"Do you recall the names Theresa Carpenter and Sarah Beers?" Brick asked.

Buckley blinked.

"I don't believe so, but I can't be sure. I meet a lot of people."

"Yeah, but you and Zack Baxter went out for drinks with these two after a writers' group meeting a few years back," Brick replied.

Baxter shot Ransom a steely look.

"I went to a lot of events when I was just starting out, I can barely remember the majority of them, let alone the names of the people I met there," Buckley said as his eyes briefly darted back toward Beverly Pepper. "I'm almost afraid to ask what's become of the two women you're asking about."

"They're both dead," Brick replied.

"How did I know that would be your answer?"

Brick shook his head. "I have no idea sir. That's just what I know."

"Do I need to get myself a lawyer before I say anything else?"

"I don't think so. I don't have plans to question you about either of these cases, not yet anyway, and I'm not charging you with any sort of crime."

"Good," Buckley replied, "cause I had nothing to do with whatever happened to those girls."

He didn't know why, but Brick was inclined to believe him.

"What happened to them?" Buckley asked after a moment's hesitation.

"To be honest, I don't really know. It doesn't look like anyone was looking into their deaths before I came along. As far as SPD was concerned, they were accidents. We may need to reevaluate that now."

Buckley completed his signature with a flourish and slid the book back to Ransom, who spun it around and flipped to the inscription:

"To my own Philip Marlowe. Enjoy the chase. - Daniel Buckley"

Brick nodded in approval and picked the book up, waving it ever so slightly in his hand. "I really appreciate this," he replied.

"I'm glad you're happy with it," Buckley replied. "But next time you're in the vicinity of a book event, or my home, could you do me a favor and call first?"

Brick nodded. "I read you loud and clear." He handed Beverly Pepper a card as he started to leave. "Ms. Pepper, if you or your brother ever need an in with the Seattle police, please give me a call. I'd be more than happy to help."

"Thank you, Mr. Ransom," Beverly replied as she eyed the card warily, seemingly waiting for it to explode in her hands.

Brick left the store with a smile on his face. Though he wasn't sure about a suspect, his gut told him he was definitely on the right track.

~

Ransom shuffled down the store's front steps and made his way to East Pike, where he trudged up the dark street in the misting rain, replaying the book event in his head.

Barrow had sure as hell been right about Buckley's temper, but it seemed clear the girl asking the question had been spoiling for a confrontation. Brick had to wonder if getting under Dan Buckley's skin was some sort of rite of passage for the literary set.

Who knew the book world could be so damn bloodthirsty?

Between Diane Norman's attacks, Peter Cornelius' criticism, and the hostility of the supposed "fans" at these book signings, Ransom almost wouldn't have blamed Dan Buckley for going on a rampage. Then again, his job wasn't about assigning blame, it was about determining guilt. Fortunately for him, guilt was color-coded in black and white.

Brick leapt over a neon-infused puddle on the next corner and stepped out into the street as he picked up the pace. The cold and rain were getting under his skin. He suddenly wanted nothing more than a hot meal and a stiff drink. The weather was shutting down his senses and closing out the sights and sounds around him, giving him late-winter tunnel vision. Tunnel vision was the reason he didn't pick up on the tail the moment a figure stepped out of the shadows outside the bookstore and started following close on his heels between 10th and 11th. In fact, it wasn't until he stopped at the corner of Pike and 12th and was scanning the show times at The Northwest Film Forum, where a poster in the window advertised an upcoming screening of 'The Big Sleep,' that Ransom caught sight of a figure following close behind him.

A razor-thin, blond-haired woman in sunglasses and a black trench coat turned at the last moment and ducked into a doorway a quarter of a block behind him. Her hands were tucked in her pockets, her shoulders hunched, as though she was trying to duck her neck down between her shoulder blades. Brick held his gaze on the doorway for a moment, then he returned to the poster. It seemed the Howard Hawks film noir was showing that week in conjunction with Seattle's Noir City film festival. He wondered if Julie Price knew about this.

Course she knows. She's the paper's head film critic.
Either way, it might be a good option for a future date.

Brick scanned the show times, checked to be sure his tail was ready to go as well, and continued up the street. No sooner did he step back onto the sidewalk, than he saw the figure in black doing likewise. Brick walked to the corner and waited, as though he was ready to cross 12th Avenue and continue east, but when the signal switched to "WALK" he held his ground. He waited, and he waited. The "DON'T WALK" sign flashed, flashed, flashed, then went to solid red lettering. When the signal to cross Pike lit up on the opposite corner, he again held his ground. Out of the corner of his eye he could see the rain-soaked blond rocking on her heels impatiently. Brick waited until the red text started to flash, then, at the last possible moment, he darted across the street. He reached the opposite corner just as the lights changed again, giving him the all clear to continue east on the other side of traffic.

A car horn blared behind him, and he turned to see the woman in black dart through the stream of oncoming traffic in hot pursuit. Brick was halfway across 12th Avenue when he suddenly did an about face and headed quickly but deliberately back to the corner he'd just stepped off, and in so doing, steered right into the path of the woman who was following him.

"Who the hell are you?" Brick asked as the woman stopped just short of running into his chest.

She pulled off her sunglasses and stared back at him with aquamarine eyes.

"Care to have a drink?"

* * *

As luck would have it, they were half a block from one of Brick's favorite spots to grab a down-to-earth meal and a top-shelf drink. Tavern Law was a cocktail lounge slash speakeasy in the Trace Lofts building on 12th and Madison. They made some of the best classic cocktails Brick had ever overindulged in, and their food, specifically their burger with red wine onion jam, provolone, and an optional (but mandatory) portion of hedonistic pork belly, literally haunted his dreams. His second-to-last serious relationship had ended, in part, when he awoke twice in one week, weeping at the memory of that perfect burger. He'd been unable to admit the source of his anguish, so the woman in question had naturally assumed the worst: another girl. Little did she realize it was even *worse* than she had feared. Foremost in Brick's heart was not some buxom, vivacious woman, but a plump, medium-well burger.

To drink, Brick went with a White Russian, and he didn't even feel bad when his new acquaintance went with a more respectable Jack Daniels, straight up. The bartender took their orders without comment. Fortunately, Ransom had never made a "mother's milk" comment while visiting this particular establishment.

Brick took a bite of his burger and stifled a moan. He turned to his dining companion and quickly cleared his throat.

"So, what have you got for me?"

Now that she was out of the trench coat and had shaken off a layer of rain, Ransom could see that this woman was quite attractive. She had some of the most beautiful green eyes he had ever seen, nothing to rival Julie Price's baby blues, and certainly not striking enough to take his mind off the menu, but still, respectable all the same.

"My name is Sally Bartleby. David Barrow sent an email out to the old Mystery Writers group this afternoon and said we could probably find you at the reading tonight if we recalled anything from Daniel Buckley's talk a few years back."

"And I take it you remembered something?"

She nodded. "I did. Especially what happened afterward."

Brick took a gulp of his drink and lowered the glass, scowling at her over a subtle milk moustache.

"So *you* were the third group member at the Pig n Whistle that night."

Sally smiled and motioned to Ransom to wipe his lip.

"I was."

"And can you tell me anything about Buckley that you think is important?" Brick asked as he wiped his mouth with a napkin.

"About Buckley? Not much. He seemed normal enough. What I really remember was his friend Zack."

"Baxter?"

Sally nodded. "Yes. Baxter."

He hadn't expected that.

"What do you remember?" Brick asked.

"Mostly that I went home with him that night after last call."

Brick took a quick sip of his drink. "And?"

"And I saw him a few more times that winter."

Brick reached for the burger again. "Sorry if I'm being rude; I'm starving. What else can you tell me?"

Sally seemed suddenly hesitant.

Brick chewed a mouthful of burger, feeling his eyelids fluttering a bit under the aphrodisiacal influence of the perfectly prepared meat. He swallowed a mouthful of burger and chased it with a couple of fries.

Still, she didn't elaborate.

"There must be something on your mind that brought you out in this shitty weather," Brick pressed. "I've actually talked with Baxter. He seemed normal enough to me. He lives right near here in fact."

Sally nodded, "I know."

"What was he like?"

"He was kind of a cold fish," she said. "But in a real arrogant kind of way."

Brick's mind flashed to the *McSweeney's* collection on Baxter's coffee table.

"Yeah, I can see that."

"At first he was kind of fun. Certainly good looking, especially for a Seattle guy. But he was also really full of himself. Far as he was concerned, he knew more about writing than anyone. Knew more about the news. Hell, he even knew more about *driving* than everyone in the city."

Brick looked up. "Driving?"

"Yeah, he always had to make some comment about Seattle drivers."

"Oh, one of those," Brick said knowingly. "Lemme guess. Probably always had something to say about how we drive in the snow, right?"

"*Especially* in the snow." Sally said. "He was a real jackass about it too. Said he grew up in Colorado, so he was always talking about chains and driving through Wolf Creek Pass in blizzards. It got really annoying. I used to think he'd find an excuse to head to the store if it was snowing, just to prove he was better than everyone else on the road."

"He must be *loving* the weird weather we're having this

year."

"Probably," Sally replied as she reached for her bourbon. "I haven't seen him in years, but as soon as David sent out that email, that was one of the first things I thought of. Kind of funny what a person remembers."

Brick flashed to the snow-covered street with D.J. Norman's body sprawled out in the middle.

"Kind of funny what can come in handy," Brick said. "Let me ask you though. You seem hesitant to speak about this. Is there something that happened or something you know about that makes you afraid to discuss this?"

"Not specifically, no. But as soon as Dave sent out that email today, my first thought was Zack; I can never see Daniel Buckley's name without thinking of him. Between you, me, and that burger you can't stop eating, I always thought he was more infatuated with Dan Buckley than he could ever have been with me. He had a strangely possessive way of talking about that guy."

"I think I caught a glimmer of that actually. He certainly thinks highly of Buckley's writing."

"Exactly. And I admit he's good. Especially his early stuff-"

Brick had to make an effort not to roll his eyes. The Dan Buckley critiques were beginning to sound like the line about the 'early, funny' films in 'Stardust Memories.'

Sally continued, "But the thing is, he's just a mystery writer. Zack had this sort of controlling streak whenever Dan Buckley or his books came up. He really didn't like people criticizing the guy at all. Hell, he didn't even like people voicing faint praise."

"When was the last time you spoke to him?"

"Zack? Like I said, it's been years. But given what I've been reading in the news, especially after what happened to Sarah and Theresa, I wanted to be sure you had interviewed him."

"I've spoken to him once," Brick mumbled as he finished his burger and wiped his hands. "But it might not hurt to dig a little deeper and pay him another visit."

Brick had parked his car around the corner from Elysian Brewery. He was still smacking his lips at the memory of his meal, even as his mind turned the conversation over in his head. Despite the newest bits of information, Buckley and Maureen Alexander were the individuals who kept coming to mind. Yet Sally Bartleby had seemed genuinely hesitant to speak to him. Obviously something about her brief relationship with Zack Baxter had left her feeling ill at ease, particularly in light of recent events, but Ransom liked to think of himself as a fairly reliable judge of character, and his own interactions with Baxter hadn't set off any mental alarm bells. The guy gave off a distinct douchebag vibe, but that didn't necessarily make him dangerous.

Shit.

He'd forgotten to switch his phone back on after the reading.

A fine mist of icy cold rain glazed the screen as Brick took the phone from his pocket and turned it back on. The temperature was still plunging, but he didn't get the sense it was going to sleet or snow again. He sure as hell hoped not at least. He'd weathered an extended adventure in a Seattle snowstorm awhile back, and he wasn't eager to go through anything like that again!

The screen came on and a moment later the phone vibrated in his hand. Brick looked at the display and saw he had a voicemail from Flynn. He tapped the screen and brought it to his ear.

Flynn's voice crackled through the static-filled message. "Yeah, Brick. We're hearing good things on this end. Whatever you did on your date with Julie, you turned in a solid performance, or at least a halfway convincing imitation of charm. She wants to see you again, so Morgan and I took the opportunity to invite her along with us tonight for dinner at The Gainsbourg up in your neck of the woods. If you're interested in joining us for an informal second date, stop by anytime after 8."

Sweat sprang to his brow. He usually needed at least a 24-hour window before he could commit to doing anything. This was unheard of! What should he say? What would he wear? There was no way he *wasn't* going, but the pressure of doing everything just right suddenly seemed overwhelming. What would he order? He'd just had a burger, so the Gainsbourger was out. Did they still make the croque-monsieur? Would that leave him limber enough if things progressed to-

Bob Seger blared through his phone's speaker, setting his heart racing into overdrive.

He'd definitely better change his ringtone before tonight!

"Hello," he answered without looking at the screen.

"Brick," O'Brien said. "I've been trying to get through to you for the last couple of hours. Where have you been, man?"

"I was at a book reading."

"*Seriously?!* Are you doing *anything* related to this case?"

"It was for Daniel Buckley! I had a few questions for him."

O'Brien hesitated. "All right, fine. Well, while you were out hobnobbing with the vicious circle, I was getting that information you wanted. Dan Buckley definitely does not have a driver's license, and he never has. Just a state issued ID."

"OK, that's very helpful."

"And just going on something else I was curious about that might interest you: Maureen Alexander and Zack Baxter drive identical vehicles."

"Baxter drives a 2013 BMW?" Ransom sneered as he fumbled with his keys in the lock on his old cruiser. "How in the hell does he afford that?"

"Well, Alexander's is paid off. Looks like someone in Colorado is making the payments on Baxter's. Either way, going on your suggestion, some of the officers canvasing Diane Norman's neighborhood spoke to a group of kids who were up early the other morning. Couple of them thought they saw a black car driving through there when no other vehicles were out."

"I've seen Alexander's car. It's black."

"Like I said, they're identical."

The gears were churning again.

"Any idea how Beamers handle on ice?" Brick asked.

"Not a clue. You've seen what I drive. My Beamer money goes to the college fund."

Brick climbed into the driver's seat and turned the ignition. The car rumbled to life as he sat there thinking.

"Hey, O'Brien-"

"Yeah?"

He sounded a little testy.

"Any idea if the buses were running on a normal schedule last night?"

"Jesus, Ransom. How in the hell should I know? I haven't ridden the bus since 1997!"

"Could you look into it?"

There was a moment of silence, then a grumble. *"Yeah."*

"Thanks, O'Brien. That could be extremely helpful."

"What's next?"

"Next? Next I've got a hot date!"

"Of *course* you do," O'Brien muttered bitterly before he hung up.

*   *   *

Brick wasn't worried about seeing Flynn. Despite their little tiff on the phone two days ago, he knew they could brush it off unaddressed and move on. It wouldn't be the first time they had gotten on each other's nerves over the years. Flynn could take pleasure in knowing that he'd been right to put Brick in touch with Julie. Brick could take pleasure in knowing he'd made such a good first impression that Julie had convinced Flynn, consciously or unconsciously, to arrange an unofficial second date.

Usually, Ransom was no fan of the second date. If he was lucky enough to have things go well on the first go-around, he was always afraid the second get-together might inadvertently knock away his prince charming mask and expose him for the imperfect mess that he was. Kind of like the dinged paint on the oven door that reveals the avocado finish beneath.

He did not want to be an avocado oven, God dammit.

What he *wanted* was to be the Maltese Falcon. Scrape

away the brooding black coat of paint and uncover layer upon layer of fine jewels, each more bewitching than the next.

Brick Ransom was a jewel. A tough talking, fine cooking, good loving jewel. And so help him, he was gonna make sure Julie Price knew it!

Hopefully a double date as second date, with the help of his close friends to keep him relaxed and enthralling, would be a good next step. It certainly put his excited apprehension at ease, if only by a few degrees. He was ready to get in there and get to work winning that gorgeous film critic's heart and mind. He also wanted to win her hand, and of course those legs. Ah those legs…

But first he had to address a bit of a B.O. situation.

A night out, followed by an all-nighter - powered by cup after cup of coffee-fueled investigation – capped off with a bite to eat at a small speakeasy with a big-time kitchen, had left Brick smelling of caffeine perspiration, kitchen grease, and fatigue. Even *he* couldn't fool himself into thinking that his current state of grime-encased sweat-reduction would act as a powerful pheromone-infused aphrodisiac. Plainly-speaking, he was rank.

Ransom pulled off his shirt as soon as he walked in the door of his apartment. He had about fifteen minutes to get cleaned up and dart up Greenwood to the Gainsbourg. After checking the fridge for eggs and creamer (though the very thought of another cup of coffee horrified him) he hopped in the shower for a thorough scrub-down. He climbed out a moment later (making sure to hide his turquoise loofa in the cabinet), and toweled himself dry as he stole another look at the clock and zipped down the front hall to the walk-in closet. A pair of slacks and a button up shirt would be just the ticket. He grabbed a bottle of Dolce and Gabbana and sprayed it on his wrists and belly – after a moment's hesitations he leaned into the bedroom, where he straightened up the bed and sprayed another shot of cologne in the air over the sheets – then he slipped back into the closet and tucked in his shirt. He straightened all the clothes out, brushed back his close-cropped hair, slipped on his shoes, and looked at the clock again.

Ten minutes. Not too shabby.

The walk to the intersection of 85th and Greenwood gave him a chance to catch his breath as he triple-checked his pockets for his wallet and keys. His mind *briefly* flashed to the investigation at hand as he passed Neptune Coffee, the former meeting place of the Greenwood Mystery Writers Circle. He looked across the street to the Pig n Whistle, where two now-deceased members of the circle had once gone for drinks with Zack Baxter and Daniel Buckley. A horn honked and Brick returned to the business at hand, pausing only briefly to check his reflection in the windows of the antique shop on the corner. Then he crossed 85th, crossed Greenwood, and headed up the east side of the street toward the canopy with the red glass bulbs.

Like most Fridays, the Gainsbourg was jumping. Brick stepped through the curtains by the door, feeling the cold air that whooshed in with him evaporate into the atmosphere of drinks, food, and conversation. A black and white Humphrey Bogart movie flickered on the wall at the back of the room. Brick caught his breath for a moment, waiting for a sign. Then he recognized it. 'Key Largo.'

Damn.

If it had been a certain film adapted from a *certain*

Dashiell Hammett novel, he'd have taken it as one hell of a good sign.

He glanced around the room, looking for a table of three, then saw Flynn and Morgan seated facing him in a booth near the back. Brick wove nimbly through the crowd till he was standing at their table.

"Brick!" Morgan exclaimed over the noise of the crowd.

"Hi, Morgan."

"How are you-" Flynn asked.

"No Julie?!"

Morgan turned to her husband with a smile, "Wow, he really *does* like her."

Brick pulled out a chair and sat down, preparing himself for disappointment.

"Relax, buddy. She went to the powder room."

"Sorry," Brick said, realizing he had a distinct case of tunnel vision. He turned to Morgan, "Yeah, I like her," he whispered conspiratorially. Then, seeing the bump of Morgan's stomach he whispered again, "Congratulations."

"Thank you," Morgan replied as she knocked on the top of the table.

"So far so good," Flynn said as he pretended to knock on his wife's stomach.

She gave him a look.

Brick was about to say something encouraging, but he was sure they'd heard it all before, so he just smiled and nodded, hoping the expression in his eyes let them know just how much he wanted things to work out for them this time. He picked up the drink menu, and was scanning the list of specialty cocktails – *Edith Piaf, Brigitte Bardot, Jane Birkin, Gainsbarre* – when he saw Julie strolling down the back hall toward them. The bounce in her hair and the way she absent-mindedly played with one strand of curls as she wandered toward them -- he suddenly realized just how much he'd been thinking about those gestures in the back of his mind for the last twenty-four hours.

Brick got to his feet and pulled the chair out beside him.

"Good to see you," he said.

"Good to see *you,*" Julie echoed.

They smiled awkwardly before a waitress with two apple tattoos, one on each of her biceps, came strolling over to their table.

Flynn clapped his hands together. "Shall we get some drinks?"

~

The dining room had grown quieter as the night went on and the restaurant's signature absinthe-infused drinks instilled their soothing influence upon the tables of diners. 'Key Largo' was followed by 'Chinatown' on the movie screen above their table, and Jack Nicholson had just had his nostril filleted by Roman Polanski when Brick ordered the cheesecake with wild Montana huckleberries and asked-

"What's with all the detective movies tonight? They usually show foreign films here."

The evening had gone *very* well, and Julie, seductively sleepy-eyed from a plate of poulet confit and several lemon incests – a zippy concoction of citrus vodka and sparkling French lemonade – reached her arm around Brick's back. He glanced to his right as her fingers settled on his shoulder. Then he looked back in her direction, where the laconic expression in her eyes delivered an additional message along with her response.

"I think they're running them to go along with Noir City tomorrow."

"Oh," Brick wondered aloud. "Is that this weekend?"

"Yep," Julie said as her fingers twirled a lock of hair at the back of Brick's neck. "The opening gala is tomorrow night at the Seattle Art Museum."

Morgan, who was watching the relaxed body language with a noticeable hint of amusement, took a sip of tea. "I've always wanted to go to that. I think Tom Douglas does the food. It sounds like so much fun."

"Actually," Flynn interjected. "I heard Ethan Stowell is taking the catering over this year."

"Tom can't be too happy about that!" Brick said as he neared the end of his White Russian.

Flynn laughed. "The rivalry grows."

"It's always a really fun event," Julie added. "You can usually see half the people in Seattle that you're always *hoping* to catch a glimpse of the rest of the year. Eddie, Dave, Will Baker, Bill, Jeff Pepper-"

"You know, I just met his sister Beverly at an event this evening."

"I'm sure she'll be there, too. Beverly Pepper is one of the primary sponsors of the festival."

"What exactly happens at the opening night event?" Morgan asked.

"Mainly it's a meet and greet, but they always have a few rooms set up upstairs with film props and screenings of classic noir films. There are usually quite a few mind-blowingly elaborate noir-inspired art installations in the galleries as well. They recreate classic film sets and invariably pull out all the stops."

"Sounds fun," Brick said.

"You could come with me if you like," Julie offered. She turned to Flynn and Morgan, to avoid being rude. "You guys are welcome too, of course."

"We wouldn't want to horn in," Flynn said.

"I'd certainly like to try to make it to the opening if I can wrap work up on time. Hopefully I can make it through one day without someone else getting *killed.*"

Julie set her hand on Brick's cocktail glass. "You should lay off the 'mother's milk' so you'll have enough energy."

"Oh God," Flynn said. "Is that what he's been calling those damn drinks of his again?"

Morgan laughed a little as well, but changed the subject in an apparent attempt to save what she could of Brick's dignity. "What exactly is film noir?" she asked.

"It's kind of like hard-boiled fiction at the movies, right" Brick said.

Julie Price leaned back in her chair, but kept one hand rested on Brick's forearm. "In a way, yeah. I've always thought it was the sexiest genre, full of criminals and antiheros indulging their deepest desires and engaging in dark deeds in the shadows." She squeezed Brick's arm imperceptibly.

"I've always wanted to know more about that," Brick mused. "But now I'm *really* interested."

Julie laughed as she gave him a look. "I don't know about anybody else, but I have to work again tomorrow. Should we get the check?"

~

The four of them said their goodbyes out on the street, surrounded by a group who had stepped out of the restaurant for a smoke.

"This was a lot of fun," Julie said.

"Where are you parked?" Flynn asked. "We can walk you to your car."

Morgan gave her husband a look, then motioned north on Greenwood. "We're parked up the street a little ways."

Julie motioned in the opposite direction. "I'm actually parked south of 85th."

'That's right near where I live. I can walk you to your car," Brick offered.

Julie slipped her arm through the crook of his elbow. "That would be perfect."

Morgan and Flynn knew what was what. "Goodnight you guys," they said in an alternating series of farewells as Julie and Brick meandered down the sidewalk.

Julie leaned close as she and Ransom waited for the signal at the corner. "If you wanted to have a night cap at your place, I could teach you a bit more about those dark deeds in the shadows."

"That's what I was hoping you would say," Brick replied.

Brick almost never had an easy time waking up in the morning, but something about the previous night's events had given him a rare jolt of energy, like the idea of facing another day of *living* actually held an atypical degree of promise for him. A night in bed with a sensuous and welcoming woman sure had a funny way of improving a man's outlook on life and making him want to do something with his brief time on planet earth. If it weren't for romance and the need to attract mates, Ransom suspected mankind would still be wearing animal hides and hunting for grubs in rotten tree stumps. He was *confident* that love and the *desire* for love were the only factors that made human beings do anything at all to improve themselves.

Right now, Brick wanted to do something for Julie. He slipped out of bed, gingerly extracting his arm from under his companion's head. He padded into the walk-in closet and dressed in the dark.

The cold wood floors creaked under Brick's weight as he slipped into the kitchen. In the space of ten minutes, he filled a large saucepan ¾ of the way with water and placed it on the glowing back burner. Next, he sliced up what remained of the one-pot bread he had prepared a few nights back. He browned the slices in the toaster oven as he heated olive oil and a diced shallot over high heat in one of his favorite small saucepans. To that he added mushrooms and salt & pepper, heated everything through, and added a few splashes of cognac and cream, all of which he brought to a boil. After a few minutes, Ransom took the fragrant mixture and divided it between four ramekins, which he in turn topped with generous helpings of grated gruyere. He slipped each of the small dishes into the hot water bath in the large saucepan, and made himself a cup of coffee as the ramekins simmered in their bubbling hot water. As soon as the cheese was melted, and before he gulped down the last of his coffee, Brick broke eggs over the top of each ramekin, slipped the glass lid over the pot, and watched them cook under the whirling steam. When the eggs were finished, he fished them out of the pan, set two ramekins on each of two plates, and buttered the slivers of toast.

Brick wolfed down his portion of the breakfast and made sure everything in the kitchen was turned off. Just before he headed out the door, he ground fresh pepper and salt over the remaining ramekins and crossed two pieces of buttered toast just above the soft-cooked yolks. Though he wanted to be there when Julie woke up, he hoped the meal would keep everything kosher with the woman who was currently asleep in his bed. He set the dish on the dining room table, along with a note that read:

"See you at the museum tonight."

Then he headed out the door.

*   *   *

Amazingly, Julie Price wasn't the only woman on Brick's mind at the moment. Try as he might – *and by God was he trying* – his thoughts kept returning to Diane Norman and the first crime scene. Something was nagging at him, but he couldn't quite put his finger on it yet.

He passed *Luc* on the left-hand side of East Madison as he headed in the direction of Lake Washington. People were strolling past on each side of the street, heading out for a Friday breakfast. Madison Park was one of the more moneyed Seattle neighborhoods. Lot of people in this part of the city had been wise enough or lucky enough to invest in Jeff

Pepper's software company in the late 70s and early 80s. The result: They had the money and time required to indulge in many a casual weekday breakfast.

Brick had always liked this neighborhood; it had a very East coast vibe to it. Plus, he had to admit there was something about the way the people who owned homes here *lived* that inspired him to reach for something bigger one day. Truth was, he liked the neighborhood, and he loved the feel of the place, but he deeply envied the lifestyles of the people who lived here. Plus, *Luc* and *Rovers*, chef Thierry Rautureau's crown jewel restaurants, were located less than a block from one another. For food lovers, locations didn't get much better. Come to think of it, Diane Norman's place, which was just blocks from here, *would* be coming on the market eventually. He could always-

No. He was being ghoulish.

Plus, who was he kidding? Despite the unique circumstances surrounding his rise through the ranks, Brick's salary was unlikely to ever hit Madison Park heights. If he ever wanted to have a prayer of reaching the type of financial situation he dreamed of, he'd have to make some changes. But that was a topic for another day.

He drove another block and took a left onto Lake Washington Boulevard. He slowed a bit after the turn, his senses heightened as he took in the scene rolling toward him. The last time he'd been here, everything had been shrouded in a blanket of snow. Now it was a midwinter landscape of brown and grey. It took him a moment to get his bearings.

Brick slowed his car partway down the road, letting the cars behind him pass. This was where Anne and her team figured the killer had climbed out of his car, taken aim at

Diane Norman as she walked on the roadway a short distance away, and picked up the shell casings before he made a U-turn and took off.

Brick stared straight ahead, squinting as he visualized the snowy scene as it must have played out that morning just a few days earlier. He pictured the figure walking up ahead. Imagined her body as she was jolted by gunshots and stumbled in a fine red mist. Then he watched as Diane Norman fell to the pavement face first.

He put the car in park and climbed out.

The roadway was bone dry, but he could still imagine the layer of snow that had quickly blown into the ridges cut by the shooter's car tires just three days earlier. He heard O'Brien's assessment of the shooter's escape from this very point.

"Looks like the shooter's car pulled up behind her, fired off two rounds, then turned around and drove off like a bat out of hell."

Brick followed the arc of the escape car as he pictured it ripping a U-turn in the ice and snow, running up on the curb for a ways, and racing away. He turned around and was just walking toward the location of Norman's body when O'Brien's unmarked car pulled up and parked behind his cruiser.

"What are you doing here?" Brick asked.

"I was trying to get ahold of you on your phone," O'Brien replied, "but it kept going to voicemail."

Shit. He'd forgotten about giving Seger the night off.

Brick fished the phone from his pocket and turned the sound back on. "So how did you know where to find me?"

"I stopped by your building a little while ago and buzzed

your place. A young woman answered and said you'd left before she got up." O'Brien gave him a disapproving look.

"Did she sound mad?!"

"No. She seemed perfectly pleasant."

O'Brien was still giving him that look.

"I did make her *breakfast,*" Brick pleaded. Then he turned defensive. "Shouldn't you be happy I was out *working* this morning? How did you know where to find me anyway?"

"I remembered you asking about the cars and how they handled in winter weather."

Brick was impressed, but still a bit skeptical. "Yeah, but there are plenty of other places I might have gone. For all you knew I could be outside Mochy's in Ballard, crawling around on my hands and knees looking for tire marks."

O'Brien cocked his head at a skeptical angle that practically screamed, *'please.'*

"I also remembered that fancy French restaurant you're always blabbing about is just down the street from where we found Diane Norman's body."

Brick hated to think of himself as being predictable, but he let it go, opting instead to continue on to the location of the body drop. O'Brien followed behind.

"Anything more from Anne and her guys?" Brick asked.

"Nothing at the restaurant. No fingerprints. No camera footage – not that that was a surprise, given the state of that place."

"What about the blood?"

"Looks like we've got samples from two different individuals."

"So whoever went Ginsu on Cornelius' carotid cut themselves too? Any word on the knife?"

"They're certain it was the serrated steak knife from Cornelius' fajitas, but they haven't found it anywhere."

"It'll probably turn up in a back alley down the street just when it's no longer useful to us."

O'Brien nodded. "Probably."

"When you were looking at the vehicle information, did you happen to notice an address on Maureen Alexander's registration?"

"I'm not positive, but I'm thinking Belltown?" O'Brien replied in a way that sounded like both a statement as well as a question.

Brick nodded as he shuffled the pieces around in his head.

"You happen to check any of the bus schedules to Belltown, Capitol Hill, or Queen Anne?"

"Not yet, sorry. First thing on my list when I get downtown."

"So, we've got shitty roads Tuesday. Shitty roads last night. And no handle on the public transportation situation-?"

"What does the bus schedule have to do with any of this, anyway?"

"Two of the folks I'm looking at drive the same type of car. A third suspect has never had a license."

O'Brien didn't get it. *"And?"*

"Whoever killed one or both of these people chose to do it on two of the worst weather nights in years," Ransom said as he paced the location, studying the ground closely. "You know as well as I do how difficult it is to get around this city when a winter kill storm rolls in."

O'Brien was seeing the full picture now. "So unless

Cornelius' killer lived in the neighborhood, which is unlikely since the folks at the restaurant seem to know all the locals, then the killer in both of these cases, whether they're the same person or not, had to have either driven or taken public transit from another part of the city."

"Exactly. And if there's blood from two individuals splattered all over that restaurant booth, then we can assume whoever left was covered with the stuff. That alone would have attracted a lot of attention."

"Well, not necessarily," O'Brien interjected. "You ever ridden the 358?"

"Even on the 358, it would have drawn *some* eyeballs."

O'Brien shrugged, but Ransom was too busy scanning the street to notice.

"Ransom, what exactly are you looking for anyway?"

"I'm not sure, but I'll know it when I see it. Can you do me a favor?"

"I know. I know. Check the bus schedules, right?"

"If it's not too much trouble."

O'Brien shook his head and headed back to his car.

"I really do appreciate it," Brick called after him.

"Just make sure you leave your phone on," O'Brien shouted. "I don't want to have to track you down again to tell you what I've found."

Brick started to thank him one last time, but his partner had already closed his door and started his engine. Brick stood with his hands on his hips, watching him leave; then he trudged back down the street toward the torn-up area between the asphalt and the sidewalk. The tire treads had torn into the grass and flung sod and mud in a wide-spraying pattern away from East Madison. He scanned the grass as he pulled out his phone and dialed Dan Buckley's number.

"Yeah," Buckley's voice came on the line. He sounded annoyed.

"Mr. Buckley, Brick Ransom again-"

"Yep. I saw your name on the caller ID."

"Is this a bad time?"

"Yeah actually. In the middle of my morning writing. What's this about?"

"I was calling to see if you might have time to talk some more today?"

"I'm busy today."

"What about tonight?" Brick asked.

"I'll be at the opening of Noir City tonight, so no."

"Oh, well, I might actually be at that event with a date. Maybe we could sneak away for a minute and run over a couple of questions I have."

"Look," Buckley began. "This is starting to become intrusive. If you want me to come in for some sort of questioning, lets make arrangements and I will bring my lawyer, but for now, *no*. I will be at tonight's event on my own time, and I will not welcome any intrusive question-and-answer sessions during a social event."

"Fair enough," Ransom replied as his eyes wandered toward the road. He noticed a section where it appeared something hard had dug into the edge, chipping away a section of curb and exposing clean concrete. "I just wanted to see if there was something that had been overlooked." Brick crouched closer to the ground as he continued walking. Only something metal could have torn into the surface that way.

Then he saw it.

"Ransom, what the hell is this about?"

"Thank you, sir. We'll be in touch," he said as he hung up the phone.

About ten feet from the spot where the killer's vehicle had driven up on the curb, Brick spied a subtle glimmer of worn metal peeking out among an accumulation of decaying leaves and gravel. He walked over and picked it up.

The linked metal object uncoiled under its own weight as Brick raised his arm and brought it toward his face.

Ransom got to his feet and dialed O'Brien.

"Lemme guess," O'Brien asked after the first ring. "You want me to check the water taxi schedule for you too."

Brick studied the twisted, gnarled object closely. It was a broken tire chain.

"How soon do you think we can get another search warrant?"

*   *   *

Ransom got to The Madison Lofts just as the sun was threatening to drop down behind the Olympic Mountains. Getting ahold of a judge and leap-frogging through the county's warrant-issuing bureaucracy was growing more laborious each time, but he managed to obtain the paperwork he needed before the end of the business day. Still, the sky was simmering a subtle pink over the Sound as he pulled up to the building's main entrance, parked his ancient cruiser in the 30-minute loading zone, and marched up to the door. He buzzed Baxter's number once. Twice. But there was no answer.

Brick checked the call box and saw the number for Madrona Property Management posted beneath the list of residents' last names. He dialed the number and paced back and forth in front of the building. A receptionist – a lifelong smoker from the sound of it – answered just as a young couple stepped out of the building.

"Yeah, hello, my name is Detective Ransom with the Seattle Police department," Brick said into the phone as he stepped forward, blocking the door with his foot as he reached into his pocket and pulled out his wallet. He flashed his badge to the young man, who studied it in a state of mild confusion, then held the door open. Brick stepped inside as he answered the receptionist's accusation on the other end. "No, this isn't a joke. My last name really is Ransom. I'm down here at The Madison Lofts with a search warrant and it looks like I'm gonna need someone from your office to come down here and give me access to a unit."

Aside from a cute young woman in jeans and a Catwoman hoodie, who was seated on a bright orange couch checking her phone, the lobby was empty as Brick strode across the creaking floor and hit the button for the elevator. Folks were either getting ready to go out on a Friday night, or they were already at happy hours across the neighborhood.

"That would be perfect. The sooner the better," Brick said as he hung up the phone and stepped inside. He caught sight of the Catwoman girl just as the doors closed.

A Capitol Hill cutie! Might not be so bad if the Madrona folks were a smidge late getting down here.

He got off on Baxter's floor and headed down the hallway. He noted several of the units had folded sheets of paper slipped into the door jams. When he got to Baxter's place, unit 302, he found the door was completely bare. He knocked on the wood with the palm of his hand.

"Baxter, this is Detective Ransom."

No answer.

"Baxter?"

He tried the door.

Locked.

Ransom headed back down the hall, stopping for a moment to pull one of the folded pieces of paper from the nearest door and look it over. It was a flyer from the management company with today's date at the top, reminding owners that window cleaners would be at the building next week. Brick returned the paper to the door and stepped into the elevator.

Baxter had clearly been home today.

The elevator whisked him back down to the ground floor.

Perhaps Catwoman could keep him company while he waited. Girls with those Catwoman hoodies with the ears were always up for a good time.

He looked down at his phone as he waited for the elevator doors to swoosh open. He had two text messages. He swiped his finger across the screen to bring up the first. It was from Julie:

"Heading into the event. They're collecting our phones (guest of honor is a stickler about them) so I won't have it on me. I'll be around the 'Citizen Kane' fireplace in the original wing. Can't wait to see you. – Julie

Ransom felt instantly guilty for the Catwoman-loving Big Bad Wolf tone of his inner monologue. Stupid. A guy his age ought to be embarrassed for salivating over a girl a decade and a half his junior, a girl who probably had a thing for, hell, whatever he *wasn't!* What were his selling points to someone like that? 'Hey girl, I'm a cop in his early 30s, with some stubborn brie weight around the middle and a fear of knives?' Embarrassing. She probably *loved* knives. Probably had a little

Angelina Jolie/Dragon Tattoo air of danger about her, slept with a Ginsu under her pillow.

The doors opened and he saw the empty orange couch.

Dammit! But… just as well…

He crossed the room and flopped down on the couch. He brought his hand to his forehead as he struggled to process the waves of conflicting adrenaline that were undulating through his temples. On the one hand, he was anxious over this case, but on the other hand, he'd been briefly titillated by some random Capitol Hill mystery girl who he'd seen for all of a split second, and on the third hand, if he'd *had* a third hand, he realized he was still thinking about Julie Price, even when he didn't *realize* he was thinking about her. This could be interesting.

His phone vibrated. It was a text message from O'Brien.

'Buses were running on regular routes last night. And just an FYI – Just checked. Zack Baxter has no gun licensed in WA, but he did have one registered in CO.'

Good to know.

That tidbit seemed to reboot Brick's thinking--

Three likely suspects. The initial winner of the *"Most Likely to Murder"* contest being Maureen Alexander, later followed by Dan Buckley, with Zack Baxter coming from behind as an unexpected front-runner. Now it turned out that two of the potential suspects were likely armed. One definitely. The other possibly.

Could he safely wipe Dan Buckley's name from the suspect sheet?

Maybe.

Brick surveyed the lobby absent-mindedly. Now, what were the motives? Who stood to gain from two murders? If it was a matter of ego, then Buckley or Alexander fit the bill. Business and money? Probably Alexander or perhaps someone he hadn't even heard about yet. If this was a wild card case, or something involving, what? Lust? Fanaticism? Then he was probably looking at Baxter, but then again, fanaticism didn't pick just one host, it was an opportunistic virus to which anyone was susceptible.

Still, his gut was starting to point to Baxter, even if the evidence wasn't backing up a traditional motive.

Not yet anyway.

Brick eyed the wall of industrial sewing machines. He liked this type of place, even if it had an over the top hipster vibe about it. Did anyone who lived in his building even know how to thread a needle? Did it matter? Machinery was hip. Old relics and outdated knick-knacks were the stuff of steampunk hipster home paradise, right?

But who was paying for it? Why hadn't he looked into Baxter's background a little closer?

Well, O'Brien *had* poked into it a bit hadn't he? Someone else was paying the mortgage on this place, that's what he'd said. Most likely, that meant Baxter came from a family with some sort of money; 'cause Lord knew most folks in the Colorado housing market would balk at the idea of paying Seattle real estate prices if they didn't have to, especially on a place like *this*. Either they were incredibly indulgent, or they weren't accustomed to counting their beans.

What did that have to do with *this*?

Again, Brick wasn't sure. He just had a hunch about Baxter, one he attributed – fairly or unfairly – to *most* people who read Dave Eggers' twee literary publication, which itself seemed bizarrely antithetical to Baxter's usual taste for hard-

boiled fiction; they were folks with blinders on when it came
to their own indulgences, and like kindergarteners, they
didn't react well when someone appeared poised to take away
their toys.

Brick turned at the sound of a key turning in the heavy
industrial front door. It opened, and an older man, likely in
his late-70s, with a red face and a broad smile, came stepping
through the entrance toward him. He walked with a slight
limp, but his friendly expression betrayed no pain. His hand
was stretched out in greeting by the time Brick got to his feet.

"You the detective that called a bit ago?" the man asked.

"I am," Brick replied as he shook his hand and passed
him the warrant.

"Lloyd Nolte. Pleased to meet you. Sorry it took me so
long to get down here. Got a bit of a bum knee." He looked
over the warrant. "Haven't seen one of these in a while," he
continued as he held the paper at arm's length and squinted
slightly. "All right, I'll take you up there."

Baxter's loft appeared much the same as the day Brick
had stopped in to interview him. It was a wide-open space
with high ceilings held up by massive, unfinished wooden
beams. Exposed brick walls wrapped the perimeter, with
rooms walled off at either end. At one end was the entrance
to the kitchen, at the other were two doors: The door on
the right was ajar, providing a clear view into a dimly lit
bedroom. The door on the left, a plated metal number that
appeared to be original to the building, was closed.

Brick crossed the room, sneering at the pile of
McSweeneys as he passed. He leaned into the bedroom,
quickly giving the place the once-over. The bed was unmade,

the curtains drawn, shutting out what for many Seattleites would have been a highly coveted view to the west. Brick strolled over to the nightstand, where he looked over the books. Two Daniel Buckley titles, a hardbound James M. Cain collection, and a dog-eared paperback of *The Maltese Falcon.* A spiral notebook lay on the bed, a scattering of confetti dusted about, telltale evidence that a large number of pages had recently been torn out all at once. Brick picked up the much-reduced notebook. Aside from a grocery list in the back, there was nothing inside. Ransom crouched to the floor and leaned under the raised bed. Nothing. Not even a dust bunny.

Whoever paid the rent on this place must spring for a cleaning service as well.

Brick headed out and turned to the metal door. He tried the lock, but it wouldn't budge.

"Do you have a key to this room?" He asked Lloyd, who was leaning against the wall by the front door, rubbing his knee as he watching Ransom make his way around the unit.

"It should be the same as the one for the front door," Lloyd said as he walked over.

Brick watched as the property manager slipped the key from his key ring into the lock in question. Though it slid into place, when he tried to turn it, the key wouldn't budge.

"That's weird," Lloyd murmured. "This should be the one."

He tried the ones on either side of the unit's master key, but neither worked.

Brick studied the lock. It had clearly been mounted from the other side of the door, so no one from the outside could unfasten it or loosen the bolts.

"Let me just try one more," Lloyd said as he took a pass with another key.

Still no luck.

"He must have changed this one out."

"Mr. Nolte," Brick asked. "Any chance your have a crowbar around here?"

Lloyd nodded. "I have a workshop downstairs. I'm sure I've got a Wonder Bar or something."

"Any chance any of the residents have storage down there as well?" Brick asked.

"Yes. Matter of fact, every unit has a locked storage cabinet in the garage."

"Think you might be able to show me Zack Baxter's cabinet?"

"I could show it to you," Lloyd said, "But I don't know if it would do you much good. I don't have keys to any of the owners' storage units."

Brick looked down at the older man's hand as he continued to rub his knee.

"Why don't I save you the trip and get that by myself."

Lloyd handed Ransom the ring of keys. "That would be much appreciated."

*   *   *

Julie Price parked her car in the "Chicago" level of the Seattle Art Museum's underground garage. It always seemed a little funny to use the garage of what she considered one of the best art museums in the country, only to hop into the elevator and see a sign for *Chicago* to help her remember what level she had parked on. Seemed like a betrayal somehow. On the few occasions she had managed to park on the "Seattle" level she had to admit feeling a certain degree of hometown pride-

Oh shut up! It was a parking garage, nothing more.

The elevator took her to the lobby of the museum's new addition, where she stepped out into the din of excitement. The Noir City Film Festival seemed to have reached a tipping point year. The lobby was packed with a much larger crowd than in years past. While the International Film Festival got most of the headlines at the start of the summer, this more niche winter series was starting to draw bigger and bigger crowds. The spirit of overwrought danger, hard-drinking heroes, and take-no-prisoners tough-guy antics seemed to be appealing to people in today's "think before you speak" world of social and political landmines. Either that, or Seattleites were just desperate for mid-winter entertainment options. Plus, when you compared a black and white detective film with the Seattle International Film Festival's typical lineup of mumble-core hoodie dramas and slacker romances, the films with the bullets and fedoras always won out, as far as she was concerned. The opening-night gala at the museum, held the evening before the week of screenings began city-wide, had clearly assumed its place as *the* society shindig this year.

Julie looked to her left, where a series of white cars – an art installation - hung suspended over the formal crowd below. Explosions of multi-colored flashing lights shot out from the car windows, giving the impression of a film sequence depicting an automobile flipping end over end in a volley of sparks and explosions. Tonight, she noted that something seemed a bit different about the look of the place. It appeared hundreds of long strands of 35mm film, or at least, a thick material that had been made up to look like film, had been strung down from the ceiling. Additionally, it appeared as though floating streamers of the same material had been suspended from thin filaments, adding to the illusion that reels of film were unspooling and floating through the air over the crowd. Julie usually loved walking under that exhibit, and tonight she *really* wanted to see what this was about, but she also needed to get into the original wing of the museum, which, as she'd mentioned in her message to Brick, had always reminded her of the massive staircase at Xanadu in 'Citizen Kane.' The deep hall, with the wide-stepped stone staircase climbing back into the shadows, almost perfectly replicated the look of the stairs in Charles Foster Kane's final, lonely residence. It was the ideal location for a film festival celebration.

This year's guest of honor was premiering one of his films in a specially installed screening room upstairs, and being a stickler for absolute silence – he'd once gained headlines for choking a critic who answered his phone during a review screening – one condition of his agreeing to appear at the opening night event was that all cell phones, even those of the most famous of Seattle luminaries, would have to be checked at the door. Having known about this ahead of time, after sending Brick a reminder, Julie had locked her own phone in her car before heading upstairs. Judging by the backup in the new lobby, it appeared others in attendance had not gotten the memo, and in today's smartphone-addled world, people were apparently putting off going through security until the last possible moment in order to tap out their final texts and Facebook updates. Since she wanted to get into the new wing as quickly as possible to ensure she didn't miss seeing Brick, Julie slipped outside and ran down the street to the original entrance, where she slipped into line beneath The

Hammering Man sculpture as she waited her chance to pass through security and get inside.

Julie was not a fan of lines, never had been, but as a film critic, queuing up for any film-related event was particularly alien to her. Fortunately, tonight she had more on her mind than just movies.

~

Brick was not a fan of basements.

Never had been.

As a kid, he used to get sent down to the basement at family gatherings at his aunt and uncle's place. While the guests and his older relatives sat around upstairs, drinking wine and talking about the news and social gossip, Brick was banished to his uncle's den, which had a huge TV, and HBO -- two good selling points for a kid whose family had an old twenty-inch tube set and a handful of over-the-air signals -- but it also meant he had to sit alone in a sterile room with mostly empty shelves, cold slate floors, and two walls of floor to ceiling windows that looked out onto the dark nighttime woods surrounding the property.

That last part was the killer.

While Brick might have relished the chance to see a Schwarzenegger flick without his mother switching it off the moment the first villain had his head blown off, he couldn't help but glance over his shoulder every minute or so to be sure no crazed madmen were peering in the windows at him. The worst part of having to go down to the basement was the trip from the bottom of the stairs, down the long, dark hallway that ran past the storage and laundry rooms, and into the den itself.

That stretch of corridor had always had a distinct

basement *smell,* and it freaked him out.

He'd usually ran the distance at a full sprint, then jumped on the couch and stayed crouched down, hopefully out of view from the windows, while he tried to watch the show. Course, the basement smell would still drift in after him.

Dank. Dark. Mildewy.

He was *not* a fan.

As he got older, and was allowed to go downstairs with his uncle to peruse the wine cellar as the older man selected the vino for family dinners, Brick began to associate the dank smell, just a bit, with the luxury of fine wine.

Of course, no sooner would he start to think of wine, than his mind would jump to *The Cask of Amontillado* and the terrifying image of Fortunato's chained skeletal remains, bricked up behind a stone wall in catacombs beneath some unknown palazzo. Brick could almost hear the ghostly jingle of the dead man's jester's cap before his blood ran cold. On more than one occasion he had damn near dropped a case of wine as he scrambled up the stairs to get the hell away from the damp smells of that infernal basement.

There weren't too many things that scared Brick Ransom. Unexpected deaths, dancing, cooking knives (inconvenient for a self-styled chef), and dank basements seemed to top the list.

All that is to say that by the time he'd located the stairs winding down to The Madison Lofts' lower level, and caught a whiff of that dank *basement* smell, Ransom was very much on edge. He fought the urge to take out his service revolver and hold it at the ready as he slipped stealthily down the stairs. *That* would probably have been a very bad idea.

Last thing he needed was another one of his butterfingered accidental shooting incidents.

Somehow he always managed to get lucky with them, but sooner or later he was bound to miss the bad guy and end up shooting an innocent bystander.

Besides, maybe as a grown man, a cop no less, it was time to act a little tougher. When he needed to man up, Ransom always turned to a simple, foolproof mantra:

What would Martha do?

Hell, if anyone dared mess with Martha Stewart, they'd probably get a steel-toed kick in the balls a moment before she handed them their disembodied larynx. Not that anyone would ever *dare* to tangle with the unfailingly dominant domestic doyenne.

The last step creaked under foot as Brick reached the heavy metal door at the bottom of the stairs, where a sign read "Residents and Property Management Only."

Brick sorted through the keys, looking for one stamped DO NOT DUPLICATE. He found it and slipped it into the lock. The door swung open on the first attempt. The basement smell enveloped him as he stepped into a darkened corridor. Ransom placed his hand on the interior wall, willing himself to stand his ground as he lowered his head and inhaled a slow, steady breath through his mouth, filling his lungs with humid air.

Keep it together, Ransom.

He peered up and down the hallway. A sequence of bare bulbs hung from the ceiling, their glass housings encased in protective metal cages. The door to the right read: GARAGE. The door to the left read: FACILITIES.

He headed to the left and again sorted through the keys

until he found one stamped: MAINTENANCE.

A few seconds later, he was staring into an even darker, *danker* room, feeling around for a light switch to the side of the door. He swept his hand up and down the painted cinder block wall, feeling about futilely for a switch. Then he took a deep breath and waved his arms about in front of him as he stepped forward into the darkness and finally felt a metal chain graze his hand. He wrapped his fingers around the chain and pulled. The room emerged from the darkness, glowing a sickly yellow under the glare of a single bare bulb.

Brick looked around the building's maintenance shop. A workbench sat against the wall a few feet ahead of him. A sump pump rumbled in the darkness off to the side. Ransom waited for his eyes to adjust, then he took an informal inventory of the room. Hammers, screwdrivers, and a variety of blunt tools, the would-be implements of a psycho killer, hung from the far wall, their worn edges glinting out at him from the darkness.

Brick looked everything over, then he grabbed a crowbar, pulled the light chain again, and started for the exit.

Back out in the corridor, he locked the door and started for the stairs. At the last moment he reconsidered his hasty escape and chose to continue on to the garage. He'd probably have to get down there sooner or later anyway, might as well get it over and done with!

The garage was simply dreadful. Damp. Drippy. The pipes hanging from the ceiling overhead were perspiring and oozing condensation. Every other drop was followed by a cartoony *plunking* sound, like something from a Looney Tunes Merrie Melody.

He glanced around the murky catacomb of the garage.

Christ. How old was this place?!

He could practically hear Fortunato's jester's motley tinkling behind the stone wall beside him. Only a few cars were parked inside, and Brick made sure to check behind each of them for killers hiding in wait as he rushed around, looking for Baxter's storage cabinet.

Finally, at the farthest end of the garage, he found an empty parking stall marked 302, with the corresponding storage cabinet situated up against the wall at the end of the space. Brick rushed over, examining the metal cabinet. The unit was secured with a heavy metal padlock, which Ransom pulled on arbitrarily. Sucker was heavy duty.

He cased the area.

Still no one around. Aside from the plunking of dripping water, the garage was silent. Brick turned the crowbar over in his hands, hesitated for a moment as he considered what to do next, then he raised it over his head in a wide arc, and swung it down against the lock with all the strength he could muster. The crowbar *thunked* off the lock as his arm and wrist continued their downward descent.

Oof.

That hurt.

Now he was *mad.*

He considered his next move.

As the youngest child in an Irish Catholic family, Brick Ransom knew three things for certain in this world:

No one respected a tattletale.

As long as his grandmother got her Jack Daniels at 6 o'clock sharp, all was right with the world.

And if you beat on something with a crowbar long enough, eventually you could get into damn near anything.

Ransom took a deep breath, found his center, and raised the crowbar.

This was a job for the Irish method.

~

Boy was she ever glad she'd had the heads-up on the cell phone ban.

Unlike several of the famous faces walking through the security gates, Julie had not been stopped in her tracks by the virtually unheard of demand that she hand over her phone. It did seem a bit extreme, but she had to admit it was rather amusing to see the look of shocked indignation on Steve Balmer's face as he stopped to show off his new Windows Phone and was almost immediately told to write out his contact information, slip the handset into an envelope, and check it with the phone valet. If he hadn't seen Bill and Melinda checking their own phones in a moment later, Julie was pretty sure he'd have gone ballistic.

She stood on the steps beneath the Noir City banner and watched the crowd. She was there to cover the event, and though she didn't have any interviews lined up, she was still taking mental notes so she could post a little play-by-play recap on her Film Geek blog on the PI's website the next day. So, as Julie looked for her date, she was simultaneously canvasing the crowd for celebrities and Seattle notables.

Jeff Pepper was there, of course. He ate up the celebrity atmosphere and anything related to films. Undoubtedly his sister was in the crowd as well, seeing as she almost single-handedly spearheaded the event each year.

In addition to the software contingent, she saw Will Baker, Dave, and Eddie by the bar, all three of whom were dressed rock-star casual, done up in meticulously rumpled suits with open collars. Michel Renoir slipped in and out of view at one point. A week ago Julie wouldn't have given the renowned scientist a second thought, but now, knowing Brick's devotion to his brother Jean-Claude's cookbooks, she was hoping he might cross paths with her at some point so she could ask after his equally famous brother. Finally, though she couldn't see him, over the noise of the crowd Julie could definitely *hear* Jeff Bezo's distinctive laugh.

There was no doubt that there were many more powerful individuals all around her, but she couldn't place their faces. Seattle was a funny town. A lot of people here had made obscenely large fortunes by backing a few local companies at just the right moments in time, but despite having cash reserves that would make Scrooge McDuck rub his hands together as he greedily envisioned Olympic-sized money pools, most of the area's super-wealthy kept a low profile, enjoying their success, running their foundations, and keeping their eyes peeled for the next big thing. Pick a day of the week at any local coffee shop, and unless you knew them personally, you had no way of knowing if the scruffy guy in the jeans and sweatshirt next to you was an unemployed stay-at-home dad or a billionaire web founder now backing a local microbrewery.

Speaking of which, she needed a drink.

Julie was just heading for the open bar, deciding whether she wanted red or white, when a hand reached out and gently tapped her on the shoulder. She turned to see Beverly Pepper standing arm in arm with a boyishly handsome man with salt and pepper hair. An attractive red-haired woman was also with them. The other woman's taut figure made Julie question her own supple runner's physique, but just for a moment. The redhead she recognized, but she was struggling to recall her name. The man looked familiar as well. All three of them were holding champagne flutes.

"Julie, I'm so glad you could make it," Beverly Pepper said as she leaned in and gave her a European-style kiss on each cheek.

Must be all that Mediterranean cruising on her brother's yacht.

"Good to see you!" Julie exclaimed as she swept a hand around the lobby. "Bigger crowd every year, I see."

"And I couldn't be more thrilled," Pepper replied. "I believe you know Maureen Alexander from Catacomb Press."

Julie nodded and shook the redhead's hand.

That's right...

They had met about five years earlier when she'd interviewed Alexander in conjunction with the release of a film adaptation of a Diane Norman mystery.

"It's been a while," Julie said.

She had panned the movie, which had subsequently bombed.

Alexander extended a cold handshake. "Good to see you again," she lied.

"And this is one of Maureen's star authors, Daniel Buckley," Beverly continued.

That's where she knew him from! She'd seen his author photo as she flipped through a copy of one of his books at Brick's place that morning.

"Of course. I knew I recognized you from somewhere," Julie said. "The guy I'm seeing is reading one of your books right now."

Buckley laughed. "Sounds like he has good taste."

"To be honest, I think he's reading it for work."

"I hope he's not a critic as well," Alexander said.

"Actually, I think it has something to do with a police investigation."

"Oh," Beverly Pepper murmured.

The group was silent for a beat, before Buckley cleared his throat and spoke up.

"Can I ask who you're seeing?"

"Brick Ransom," Julie replied, almost apologetically turning the statement into a question.

Buckley and Alexander cleared their throats.

"Small world," Buckley muttered.

Julie's eyes moved from one to the other, then over to Beverly.

"I feel like I said something wrong."

"Not at all," Maureen said. "Just a bizarre coincidence."

Buckley motioned to Maureen with his champagne flute. "Maureen and I were just comparing notes over which of us we think your boyfriend suspects of murder."

Julie nodded, at a loss for what to say next. "OK then, maybe I should-"

She was interrupted by the quiet chirp of a cell phone. Beverly Pepper reached into her purse.

"How in the hell did you get your phone in here?" Alexander demanded. "They said it was strictly against the rules."

"When you're picking up the tab for an event like this, you set your own rules," Pepper replied as she turned away and answered her phone.

~

After a good five minutes of full-on smashing, something

inside the padlock's housing made a distinct *chunking* sound. Brick took the crowbar, set it into the lock's metal U, braced the end against the cabinet, and pulled up with all of his strength.

After a brief struggle, it popped open.

Ransom slipped the lock from the latch and threw it to the side. No sooner did he swing the doors open, than he was staring into a largely empty cabinet filled with a few random tools, half-empty containers of anti-freeze, and there, hanging off a hook in the back, three winter tire chains. They were the exact same style and brand as the one he'd found in the gutter a short distance from the Norman murder scene.

~

The elevator doors opened in the lobby of the museum's new addition, and Zack Baxter stepped out into the crowd. He marched up the steps and stopped short as he saw the crowds of people backed up at the security gates. The line-up of guests shifted back and forth restlessly under the cars and flashing lights overhead. He noticed what appeared to be swirling streamers of motion picture film floating in the air above the crowd. The dangling black strands emanated from the darkened second floor balcony, where flickering reflections, as if from motion picture projectors, seemed to backlight the eerie celluloid tendrils snaking through the air. Baxter followed the streamers of film back down to the waiting guests. From the look of things, the queue into the gala was backed up for at least an hour. That was, assuming they were still letting people in at all.

He looked past the lines to the security gates, and crossed his arms gingerly as he unconsciously ran his fingers over the weight zipped into his coat pocket. Then he noticed a young girl, about ten years his junior, standing guard in front of a barrier at the bottom of the pair of escalators that led to the exhibition floors upstairs. The usual entrance to the galleries had apparently been roped off for the evening's events. The girl was brushing her fingers through her hair self-consciously as she watched the partygoers lining up.

Baxter took a deep breath, doing his best to calm his nervous anticipation in an effort to turn on the charm, if only briefly.

He walked over to the girl, flashing a wide smile as he did his best to seem sheepish. Her face flushed the moment he began to speak to her.

"Excuse me. I hate to ask this, but I work for the catering company and I'm running a little late. Do you think there's any way I could slip into the exhibition hall this way without anyone seeing? If my boss finds out I was late again I'm a goner."

She glanced over her shoulder, then up the escalator, where the flickering lights and streamers receded into the darkness. Assured that she wasn't being watched, the girl reached over, undid the clasp on one of the velvet ropes, and waved Baxter through.

"Go ahead."

"Thanks a million," he whispered as he slipped past her and disappeared in the dark.

~

Lloyd was sitting on the sofa reading a copy of *Cheap Thrills* when Ransom walked in the door, the tire chains in one hand, the crowbar in the other.

"You read anything by this Buckley guy?" Lloyd asked. "The flap says he's local."

"That's what I've heard," Brick replied as he set the chains on the dining room table.

Lloyd got to his feet with a groan, shifting his weight to one leg as he rested a hand on the arm of the couch and rubbed his knee with the other.

"You don't think Baxter is into some sort of trouble, do you? He's always seemed like such an agreeable kid."

Brick was only half paying attention as he crossed the room, his eyes fixed on the locked door.

"I think we'll know soon enough, Lloyd."

He placed the split end of the crowbar into the gap between the door and the frame and wedged it into position with his shoulder.

"Try not to do *too* much damage!" Lloyd exclaimed just as Brick grabbed the metal bar with both hands and shoved it to the side with the full weight of his body.

The doorframe crunched under the force, wood splintering to the sides as Ransom pulled the bar back toward his body, repositioned it, and heaved it forward again. The metal caught on the edge of the now exposed deadbolt and carved a path through the remaining wood. He leaned the tool against the wall, grabbed the doorknob, and twisted it to the side as he took a deep breath.

If that didn't do the trick he could always go back to the Irish method.

He rammed his weight against the door once. Twice. The frame finally gave way with a resigned crunch, and the door swung inward.

It took a minute for Ransom's eyes to adjust to the darkness inside. He found a switch and turned on the lights. It was another few moments before the images before him began to make sense. He was in an office lined with shelf after shelf of books and journals. Again, a nice setup, seemingly well beyond the means of an unemployed guy Baxter's age. It all would have fit perfectly in the pages of some sepia-toned, yuppy hardware catalog, except for the photos and newspaper clippings taped along the shelves and on every inch of exposed wall space, which gave the place a certain serial killer *je ne sais quoi.* It wasn't a John Malkovich 'In The Line of Fire' level of crazy, but it held its own.

Brick scanned the strangely systematic explosion of taped clippings, each of them marked with red lines, circles, and strangely underlined sections of text. The best Ransom could tell, the materials went back several years. There were images of a younger looking Dan Buckley. Shots of Buckley at a book signing with a young Baxter and a remarkably unchanged Maureen Alexander flanking him on either side as they handed him copies of *On The Money* and collected the signed editions. There were articles about Catacomb Press. Shots of Buckley and D.J. Norman, then a string of shots of Norman in earlier years, along with a photo that could have been taken the week before. Some of the pages were torn in half. Some were torn and taped back together, intentionally askew. Many of them had Norman's face slashed out with red ink or dark black circles swirled over and over across her face.

Ransom noted another section that looked to be nothing but printed webpages of reviews posted on retail websites. Randomly highlighted and underlined sections formed almost mathematical patterns in the sheets of words.

Beneath those were the images of Peter Cornelius. A *Pacific Northwest Magazine* profile. Cornelius' regular book columns, profanity scrawled across each and every page. Brick recognized a copy of Cornelius' final review, the one they'd found jammed down his slit throat.

Finally, his eyes settled on a series of *Seattle Magazine* event photo spreads, filled with images of the area's rich, powerful, but not necessarily famous, all decked out in distinctly *un*Seattle style, attending various charity events around the city. Brick always found those spreads a curious specimen in the decidedly unsociety-conscious Emerald City. He supposed they made money for the magazines, as the folks who threw the fundraisers in question usually owned the car dealerships and internet companies that threw the events being covered, and advertised in the following pages. The least a regional publisher could do was run some glossy photos to make the people photographed therein feel like regional notables.

'Course, here and there Brick did see some genuinely famous faces. There were Bill and Melinda. There was Jeff Pepper with the head of his foundation and only sister, Beverly, who Jeff had just met the day before. At least, he thought it was Beverly Pepper. It was hard to tell, seeing as his face had been scrawled out by a heavy black swirl of ink, applied under such force that the page had been torn as the pen's metal tip dug into the paper. There was another image, and another, all of them showing Beverly Pepper on the arm of a well-dressed and boyishly handsome man: Daniel Buckley.

Brick leaned in closer to read a section of underlined text printed below a photo of a crossed-out Beverly with her arms around a very smiley Dan Buckley. They were photographed on the deck of what looked to be one hell of a massive estate. It clearly wasn't the house on Queen Anne that Brick had visited a few days ago. Beneath Beverly's slashed-out image was printed a quote:

"I'm trying to convince Daniel to retire so we can write a fairy tale ending together."

Jesus. Talk about your cornball nonsense.

Brick leaned back, slightly repelled by the saccharine tone, but he supposed it was a nice enough sentiment. 'Course, the *X* slashed across Pepper's heart certainly went a long ways towards counteracting any sugary-sweet symptoms. And if any uncertainty about Baxter's feeling towards Ms. Pepper remained, the next picture put them to rest once and for all.

It was a shot of Beverly Pepper standing on the steps beneath the Hammering Man statue outside the Seattle Art Museum. The article was a profile of her support for the Noir City Film Festival, and while this was the only image in which her face had not been slashed and shredded virtually beyond recognition, the gun sight etched between her eyes in red Sharpie did little to alleviate any sense of hostility.

Brick stepped in closer as he read a section of roughly underlined text:

"Just as in years past, Beverly Pepper will be the seldom recognized but most powerful name in the room at the opening of this year's Noir City Film Festival."

The floor creaked behind him as Lloyd peered in over Brick's shoulder.

"I always knew that kid was bad news."

For a well-publicized event with so many high-profile guests in attendance, the security was embarrassing. Once he'd gotten past the girl on the lower level, no one had given Zack Baxter a second glance.

Black and white, noir-inspired film installations had been set up throughout the galleries on the second floor. Several of them involved sequences of shadowy figures following men in hats and trench coats as they led damsels in distress through dark streets and back alleys. Baxter had no problem ducking into one of the displays, where he passed the shadowy outlines of guests, their footsteps echoing on the hardwood floors as they took in the shadowy, highly disorienting imagery. The viewers in the largest of the galleries were so distracted by the film's soundtrack of shoes walking on damp cobblestone streets, accompanied by jarring music and the sounds of their *own* footsteps, that no one appeared to pay him the slightest attention as he cut through the exhibits and emerged in one of the back halls. Once he crossed the threshold into the original wing, leaving the newer half of the building behind, Zack slipped into the southeast stairwell and descended several flights of stairs, till he reached the lowest level.

He'd visited the museum twice in the last month. Once last week to make sure he had the layout straight in his mind, and again just the day before, to be sure nothing had been altered so drastically for the event that he wouldn't be able to find his way in and out of the building. Aside from a number of over-the-top design elements, most notably a 'Sunset Boulevard'-inspired body floating in a pool of bloodied water, which had been situated at the bottom of the long flight of stairs, the majority of the design touches for the opening gala were derived from lighting and large banners suspended from the walls. The biggest obstacle in getting to his target would be avoiding the throngs of guests as they worked the room. There was certainly the risk of collateral damage.

Baxter stepped out of the stairwell on the lowest level and strolled down a service hallway. He could see the flashing, swirling lights of the event dancing amongst the partygoers just through the doorway at the end of the hall. His hand instinctively returned to the heavy weight in the inside pocket of his coat. He winced as his bandaged fingers brushed against the handle, sending jolts of searing pain racing from the ragged gashes in his hand. He needed stitches, but he couldn't risk going to the ER. Not last night anyway. And certainly not anytime in the near future. If it was still giving him trouble after this was all over, he'd try to get it looked at someplace across the state line. That is, assuming he moved fast enough to get out of this place alive once he'd accomplished what he had come here to do.

Long after he was gone, and long after *Dan Buckley* was gone, the work would live on. If for nothing else, perhaps he would find his way into the footnotes of a great man's life story. Whether that be as someone who enabled his legacy, or someone who had cut it short, would be decided shortly. He hoped he could avoid disaster, and ultimately be seen as a guardian of the work. Someone who played a deciding role in determining whether the writing died or thrived. He was certainly hoping for the latter – after all, Dan was not his target - but he was more than prepared for things to play out either way.

He was out in the open, weaving through the oncoming

crowd. His eyes scanned the faces of the excited guests. Then, at the foot of the imposing mass of stairs, Zack caught sight of Dan Buckley sipping wine with Maureen Alexander, a young woman with light-brown almost dusty-blond hair, and last but not least, Beverly Pepper.

If he had his way, within the next few minutes, at least one of them would be dead.

Brick rushed out of the apartment, leaving Lloyd behind to lock the place up. He punched Buckley's number into his phone, letting it ring as he ran for the elevator and pounded on the down button. The call went to voicemail as he heard the elevator ping on the floor above his, then continue climbing.

He'd have to take the stairs.

Ransom looked to the end of the hall, where he saw a placard with the image of a stick figure descending a flight of stairs. He rushed to the door, throwing it open as he hit redial. The call once more went unanswered before going to voicemail.

Baxter reached into his pocket and wrapped his hand around the gun's handle. His index finger slid over the trigger as he lifted its weight, slipped off the safety, and gently removed the weapon from his inside pocket. It felt cold, and heavy, and powerful. He kept his hand inside the front of his coat as he watched the crowd, his eyes wavering back and forth excitedly as he singled out Beverly Pepper. Dan Buckley was close beside her, talking to Maureen Alexander and the other woman, who was playing with her hair absentmindedly as she spoke. If there was one person he *didn't* want to hit, it was Dan, but if that happened, so be it. Might even be for the best. A dead author's legacy was so much easier to reshape if their published works were still relatively respected. Better to jump the tracks at full steam than lurch to the station and rust on the rails.

If Buckley stayed with Beverly Pepper, if she convinced him that living off her fortune would make him happy, then the indignities of D.J. Norman's literary eviscerations, and the critical flagellations of mean-spirited hacks like Peter Cornelius would seem justified. A potentially great writer willing to subvert his talent for the sake of living like a kept man – he was as good as dead anyways, right? Either way, he was here for the sake of the legacy; how he would shape it remained to be seen.

The majority of the group had their backs to him, which suited Baxter's purposes just fine. He stepped forward, ready at any moment to shoot any or all of them dead, one after the other if need be. He paced quietly through the passing revelers, the sounds of their voices, the liquor on their breath, the exuberant glints in their gleeful eyes, all fading into the background as he heard only the sounds of his breath and his own steady heartbeat.

Maureen Alexander, his former employer, was the first to see him coming. She was standing at the edge of the 'Sunset Boulevard' pool, and looked up, her head cocked at a curious angle as she made fleeting eye contact with him. He could see her lips mouthing the question, 'Is that Baxter?' even as her eyes went wide at the light glinting off the edge of the object he was pulling from his coat. She flung her drink to the side as she threw her arm out and tried to shove Dan and the rest of the group into the safety of the crowd. Why she didn't think he would fire into a mass of strangers was a mystery.

Zack ripped his bandaged hand from his coat and swept his arm forward, raising the handgun and taking aim at the back of Beverley Peppers head. Dan turned at the last moment, following Maureen's horrified gaze. He shoved his date to the side, even as Maureen Alexander lunged forward and knocked him out of the way.

The gun hammered into the palm of Baxter's damaged hand, the muzzle stuttering under the recoil as a red haze burst from Maureen's left shoulder. She stumbled backwards as the crowd screamed and scattered. Alexander staggered backwards, her good arm flailing as she plunged into the pool. Water from the shallow pool sloshed out onto the marble floor, where Dan Buckley was crouched on one knee, shielding Beverly Pepper. The other woman ran toward the two of them as Zack opened fire once again. The woman grabbed Dan's shoulder and pulled him to his feet. They struggled to gain their footing on the slippery stone.

"We've got to get out of here!" Julie screamed over the chaos.

Buckley's face shook as he whipped his head around in panic. Then he yanked Beverly to her feet, and the three of them took off running up the long flight of stairs.

Baxter lunged after them, but lost his footing on the drenched marble floor and went down hard. He felt something in his knee crack, but struggled back to his feet, even as his leg throbbed from the impact.

His target was getting away.

Brick ran through the lobby of The Madison Lofts, damn near knocking over a couple in matching hoodies as he threw open the double doors and raced to his car. He climbed into the driver's seat and fumbled to get the key into the ignition. His phone started ringing. He looked at the screen as he started the cruiser.

206 area code, but he didn't recognize the number.

He answered anyway.

"Yeah, Ransom here."

"Brick!" The voice screamed through the phone at him-

"Who is this?"

The radio crackled to life as the engine took hold.

"All cars, we have reports of shots fired-!!!"

Brick reached over to turn down the volume.

"Who is this" Brick repeated.

The voice on the end of the line was hushed at first, then it came through in a sharp hiss.

"It's Julie." Brick's heart dropped. "I'm calling from Beverly Pepper's phone. We're at the museum. Some guy just started shooting. He's after us-"

"Are you all right?!" Brick shouted.

The phone cut out and came back in.

"I'm with Beverly Pepper and Daniel Buckley. He's shooting-"

"Who is shooting? Julie! Who is shooting?!"

The phone cut out and in again. "-after us and-"

"Who is it?!"

Ransom heard a man's voice hissing in the background. It sounded like Dan Buckley saying something, saying-

"It's Zack Baxter!" Julie screamed as the signal broke through.

"That's what I was afraid your were gonna say. Listen, Julie, see if you can-"

The phone beeped as the call dropped.

"Hello?" Brick shouted again as he yanked the shifter into drive, stomped on the accelerator, and peeled away from the curb in a thick cloud of tire smoke.

The phone went silent. Julie glanced at the screen, praying that it hadn't died:

Signal lost.

Damn thick museum walls.

They were in an alcove off one of the second-floor corridors. Guests rushed past as they fled the galleries-turned-screening rooms, panicked by the sounds of screaming echoing up from the lower level.

"Don't come this way!" Julie yelled as a well-dressed group rushed towards them. "Someone has a gun downstairs!"

"What's happening?" someone called back, but the question went unanswered.

Just what in the hell *was* happening?

She looked at Buckley.

"So you know that guy then?"

He nodded.

"Any idea why he'd want one of us dead?"

"Not in the slightest," Dan replied. "But it seemed to me he was aiming for Beverly."

"Looked that way to me too," Julie muttered. She could hear screams emanating again from down the corridor. Whatever this guy Baxter wanted, from the sound of things, he was back on his feet and coming after them. "We'd better keep moving," Julie said as the three of them ducked into one of the now empty, pitch-black rooms.

~

Brick had the accelerator smashed to the floorboards as he roared down the hill toward downtown. His phone was clenched in his fist and pressed against his ear as he gripped the steering wheel with his right hand.

O'Brien answered on the first ring. "Yeah."

Sirens were blaring in the background.

"It's Baxter." Brick shouted. "Get to the museum. It's *Baxter!*"

"Call just went out. I'm on my way there now."

~

The three of them rushed into the next gallery, just as the film being projected across the room came to an abrupt stop and the room went completely black. The light was extinguished so quickly that none of their eyes had a chance to adjust to the darkness. Julie felt Dan Buckley's hand on her wrist as he felt around through the blackness.

"Beverly?"

"Julie," she gasped.

"I'm here," Beverly Pepper's voice whispered a short distance away.

"Can either of you see *anything?*"

"Blind as a bat, and I don't have radar," Beverly hissed.

They heard the patter of leather heels on marble. A sort of shuffling sound, like someone doing their best to soften their footfalls and not make a sound.

Baxter.

His footsteps passed the far end of the room, the direction from which the three of them had first entered. From the sound of things, he was passing them by, moving on to another gallery. Julie could *hear* the sounds of her companions holding their breath for as long as possible, before exhaling in leaking gasps, and inhaling again over dry throats.

Something on the wall directly behind them, at a 90-degree angle from the entrance, made a soft ticking sound, like a mechanism engaging.

The soft footsteps in the hallway stopped.

Tick

The sound came again. This time Julie recognized it. It was something she had heard a million times before.

The footsteps shuffled closer.

"What is that?" Dan whispered.

Julie didn't answer. The air shifted subtly. Baxter was in the room with them. If they could wait him out, if somehow, by the grace of God, they could manage to avoid running into him, or at least slip out of the room before his eyes adjusted to the darkness, they might still have a chance to escape. But she knew the sound they were hearing, and there was a pretty good chance that-

Tick – whumwhumwhum…whum…whum…whum… whum-

A blazing white light shot through the air over their heads as a projector in the wall behind them sprang to life, its gears whipping into a frenzy as the reels began spinning wildly. Ralph Meeker appeared on screen.

Kiss Me Deadly!

Julie's head whipped to the side, where Baxter was standing in the middle of the room, his arm reflexively pulled over his eyes as he swept the gun up and started to fire.

Bullets sprayed the floor, tracing their way up the wall before they hit the projector lens, sending a spray of glass and sparks exploding into the air, briefly illuminating the exploding cloud of unspooled film just before the room again went dark.

She felt Buckley's hand on her back. From the sound of things he was nudging Beverly Pepper on her way as well. Normally, Julie resisted being shoved around by a man. Of course, normally she loved that old Mickey Spillane Mike Hammer movie too, but she'd been more than happy to see it explode before her eyes, even if it meant she was now running full throttle through an ink-black haze.

In the freeze-framed image of the room that stood burned on the insides of her eyelids, Julie could picture the doorway on the opposite end, and from the feel of things, that's where Buckley was guiding them. They ran forward till her shoulder smashed into the doorjamb and she fell sideways. She felt Buckley's strong hands grabbing her by the shoulders, steadying her as he led them into the next room. This one was even darker than the last.

"Terrific," Beverly hissed, "I can't see a damn thing in here either."

~

Brick hadn't lifted his foot off the gas since he left Baxter's condo. The engine under the hood of his father's old cruiser roared, emitting a sound somewhere between a scream and a howl. He gripped the wheel and dodged traffic on Union as he raced toward the water. At the last possible moment he whipped the steering wheel to the left, his tires squealing wildly as he turned onto Third. The car's back end swept around behind him. From the corner of his eye, Ransom saw one of his hub caps break away and skitter over the asphalt surface, sparks shooting off to the sides as it shot toward the sidewalk and hopped the curb, headed straight for a bearded fellow in a plaid Utilikilt, who leapt into the air in a panic, his ill advised, traditionally worn man-skirt continuing to float upward, even as he cleared the out of control metal disc and headed back down to earth. Brick's eyes shot back to the road, but not before he'd seen everything God had given that absurdly clad gentleman.

Horrific.

He took a right at the next corner, turning into oncoming traffic and ripping the steering wheel clockwise. The passenger-side mirror dug into a row of parked cars, shrieking through metal and glass, before tearing loose and disappearing among the wreckage as the cruiser continued on. Just before he hit 1st Avenue, Brick steered the vehicle to the right, jumping the curb and smashing into a knee-high concrete wall before he slammed on the brakes. He nearly avoided the museum's towering Hammering Man statue, but was about six inches shy of clearing the enormous steel sculpture on the left. The driver's side fender crunched into the Man's thick back heel and split to the sides like soft butter.

Brick climbed out of the car and turned to see O'Brien standing at the main entrance, his jaw hanging open, his cell phone in his hand. He shook his head slowly just as Brick's phone began to ring.

Ransom glanced down at the screen before he answered, even as he saw O'Brien bringing his own phone to his mouth

"Yeah?" Brick said as he answered the call.

"I was just letting you know I'm here," O'Brien said through the headset. "But I see you've made your usual entrance."

One of the SPD officers already at the scene greeted them in the lobby. Brick recognized Matt Vanderburg from the Norman crime scene just three days earlier. He'd only had a couple of interactions with the thin, blond-haired officer over the years, but from the little he'd dealt with him, Brick was sure of two things: Officer Vanderburg liked a well-kept moustache. And he hated chaos.

The scene in the lobby was nothing if not chaotic. Guests in suits and party dresses were standing along the perimeter, clearly upset by whatever had just taken place. Paramedics were attending to someone on the floor beside a shallow pool. A red cloud swirled in the water. Blood was streaming across the floor.

"Gunman came in and just started shooting," Vanderburg reported. "Don't know for sure how he got in, but a few of the guests said they saw him entering the lobby from the service hall to the left of the stairs."

Brick followed the officer's chin as he nodded in the direction of the stairs.

"Any fatalities?" O'Brien asked.

"Woman over there was hit in the shoulder, but she's stable."

Brick looked over as the paramedics brought an oxygen mask up to the woman's face. It took him a second to recognize her with soaked hair and that pained expression, then he got a clear look at her legs and knew who she was immediately.

Maureen Alexander.

She caught sight of Brick as he and O'Brien headed towards her and motioned for the EMT to remove the mask.

Brick set his hand on her shoulder as she clenched her teeth and fought to speak through the pain.

"Baxter," she gasped.

Ransom nodded and reached down to squeeze her hand. "We know. We'll get him."

He and O'Brien headed up the stairs, skipping every other step till they reached the back of the second floor, where they stopped at the door that exited to the next level.

Brick rested his hand on the handle as he peered through the door's portal window and into the corridor on the other side.

"You ready?"

"Ready as I'll ever be." O'Brien was already pulling his gun from its holster. "If you think you can manage it, can you try not to have any of your Butterfinger moments with the trigger this time?"

Brick shot him a look as they stepped out into the shadows. He took out his phone and dialed Beverly Pepper's number.

Steadied now and holding her breath, Julie Price reached out her hands and felt her way through the pitch-black gallery, steeling herself for the moment another projector might spring to life without warning, setting them dead center in the middle of a virtual spotlight. Either that, or their pursuer would just start firing at them blindly from the darkness.

They heard no sounds coming from behind them as the group of three continued forward, but she knew he was back there somewhere, probably doing exactly like them, holding his breath and trying like hell not to make a single, solitary sound. Now and then, she, Buckley, and Beverly would brush hands as they gauged where they were and tried to stick close together.

Then they started to hear things.

The first was a heavy banging sound, which came from far behind them, back in the direction from which they'd first entered the floor of galleries. Then another noise echoed from the opposite direction, from up ahead, the sounds of a self-playing piano just beginning to tickle its own ivories.

They once more stood frozen in place as they oriented themselves to the sounds of the piano playing. It was soft, melodic, melancholy, sort of south-of-the-border music. Julie recognized it from somewhere, an old Henry Mancini piece? She could picture the movie, but couldn't quite see the faces of the stars. Something in the film noir style of course, with plenty of silence and sudden moments of-

A marimba ringtone broke the silence.

"Shit!" Beverly hissed as she scrambled for her phone.

Before it could ring a second time, gunshots once more rang out. Julie and Dan Buckley took off running as the sharp crack of gunfire echoed in the room. Julie turned, and through strobing muzzle-flashes, saw Baxter crouched to one knee, aiming for them.

Two shots.

Then a third.

On the third shot Julie dove around the corner and into the next room. She peeked around the edge to see Baxter running toward them, even as Beverly Pepper ran back in the direction from which they had just come. Pepper threw her phone to the side, diverting Baxter's fire as she raced into the darkness.

Julie turned and saw Dan Buckley leaning against the doorframe on the other side of the entrance. She looked around the room, which, like the galleries before it, was dark and disorienting, but there was a dim glow of light. A haze of theatrical smoke hung in the air, and the soft sounds of the piano still floated around them, tinkling in time to the movements of a series of throbbing, thumping pistons – *oil pumpjacks?!* – that shifted back and forth overhead. Just as she identified the music, a voice boomed out from unseen speakers; Orson Welles, muttering angry condemnations about "that Mexican – Vargas."

Touch of Evil.

This gallery, the entire massive space, had been constructed to resemble the location of the final scenes of that immortal border-town potboiler.

Footsteps thundered toward them. Julie gauged Buckley's location. No way in hell either one of them could step across that doorway without getting shot dead. She looked at him, he met her gaze, and with an exchange of nods, they each spun around and went their separate ways.

-

Brick and O'Brien heard the gunfire and took off running. The second floor was black as night, and they ran into more than a few knee-high gallery benches lurking in the shadows along the way. Damn things were at just the right height to cripple a man if he hit it the wrong way, which *both* of them managed to do.

They were feeling their way through the end of the first gallery when a woman rushed around the corner and into Brick's arms. She stifled a scream as he grabbed her and tried to calm her.

"Relax, relax," he whispered. "We're with the police."

He heard her uncertain voice, "Detective Ransom?"

It was Beverly Pepper.

"Beverly!" Brick exclaimed. "Are Dan and Julie OK?"

"So far. I think."

"OK," he said as he looked toward O'Brien's silhouette, then back to Beverly Pepper. "Stay here, and don't move. We're gonna get him."

Pepper's silhouette nodded in understanding.

They had to get him.

He couldn't bring himself to imagine anything happening to Julie.

For a recreation of a film set from an almost 60-year-old B-movie, whoever had overseen this installation had done one hell of a good job. It truly *felt* like they had been transported to the garbage-strewn stretch of border town from the finale of Orson Welles' overlooked masterpiece. The last Julie had seen of Dan Buckley, he was scaling a rusted chain-link fence behind a laundry line sagging under the weight of white, flapping bed sheets. Buckley had looked back at her from the top of the fence, given her a nod of 'good luck,' then dropped out of sight on the other side.

Julie looked around the room, her eyes growing more accustomed to the dim lighting, and saw a footbridge crossing over a pool of glimmering water. She raced over the bridge and dropped down behind a crumbling stucco wall, just as Zack Baxter emerged from the darkness, and a projector blinked to life off in the distance. A beam of light shot across the gallery, highlighting the specks of dust floating in the air, before an enormous projected image flickered and danced to life on the far wall. Then, the finale to *Touch Of Evil* began to play above them. Orson Welles' puffy face gazed down over the sprawling gallery space, watching, like a bloated frog, as life once again imitated art.

Julie pressed her back against the wall, trying her best to disappear into the shadows. From the sound of things, Baxter hadn't budged since he had set foot in the gallery. He'd probably been letting his eyes adjust to the darkness before the movie came back on and forced his pupils to clamp up tight. On the screen above, Welles' crooked police captain, Hank Quinlan, was walking through a seedy western wasteland, drunkenly confessing his indiscretions to his trusted right-hand man, who he didn't realize was wearing a wire, as Charlton Heston followed behind them, crawling under oil pumpjacks and through filthy ditches and garbage-strewn streams, all the while carrying a wireless reel to reel recorder, getting every incriminating word down on tape. On screen, Heston was just passing a thumping pumpjack, when Julie heard the crunch of gravel a short distance away, then saw Baxter heading in the direction Dan Buckley had just gone. She held her breath, waiting until the footfalls had receded a ways, then dropped to her hands and knees and crawled across the bridge. She kept crawling, even as she heard the rattling metal sounds of Baxter scaling the chain-link fence.

Ransom's head whipped around at the sound of clanking metal. It couldn't have come from too far away. Just one or two gallery spaces over. They'd left Beverly Pepper huddled in a darkened alcove where, barring some highly unlikely scenario in which Baxter circled back, they could be sure she'd be safe until this was over.

The pale green glow from an exit sign highlighted the contours of his partner's face. The whites of O'Brien's eyes darted in Brick's direction, as he signaled he was going one way, and Ransom should go the other.

Brick nodded and raised his firearm as O'Brien kept close to the wall and silently disappeared around the far corner. Brick adjusted his grip on his weapon, feeling the palm of his hand getting a familiar and entirely unwelcome clamminess. That hadn't happened in a very long while, and when it did, it usually meant he was taking things personally. In this case, that was undeniably true. Unfortunately, as he'd learned numerous times over the years, not only did clammy hands mean he was deeply invested in the outcome of whatever violent scenario was about to play out, it also meant he was much more likely to have one of his butterfingered handgun mishaps, and while so far those accidental shots had always turned out for the best, this was the first time someone he cared about, maybe even loved, just might get caught in the path of his bullet.

Keep your wits about you, Ransom boy.

Dan Buckley waited beneath the crisscrossing patterns of the metal walkways overhead, looking up through the shadows as he strained his ears for signs of his pursuer. He had just slipped from behind a towering steel oil drum when he heard Baxter jump down from the fence in the direction from which he'd just come, and he had *just* enough time to scamper to the shelter of the catwalks before he saw his former friend's backlit head pop up just to the left of a weathered shanty with a rusted corrugated roof.

Buckley kept his eyes locked on Zack Baxter's silhouette as he stumbled backwards into the darkness pooling around the metal structure of walkways and ladders that bordered the relentlessly pounding pumpjack. Buckley had just relaxed enough to let out his breath and inhale a lungful of invigorating oxygen, when he took a half-step backward and knocked an unseen metal pail off the edge of the catwalk. He winced as he waited for the recoil.

The bucket hit a metal surface below, emitting a deafening clatter, which was immediately met by the ear-splitting sounds of gunfire. Sparks exploded around him as Dan ran across the walkway, leapt back to the dirt and gravel-covered floor, and rushed across an open expanse. He flew headlong into a bed sheet, which wrapped around his head and held fast against his face as he kept running from the sounds of the gunfire and the rumble of metal and exploding wood.

He smashed into a wall, falling backwards, even as he flailed about on the ground, struggling to find his footing. Then he felt the wall before him.

Smooth gallery sheetrock.

He spread his fingers wide and followed the painted surface. He continued through the darkness, feeling his way by touch alone, till he came to what *felt* like a doorway, and he was just thinking he might have made it to safety, when two hands grabbed him from either shoulder and stopped him short. He flailed his fists in defense as the unseen hands slid down his shoulders and pressed his arms against his sides.

"Relax! Relax man," a voice murmured reassuringly from the darkness. "I'm with the police."

Buckley clawed at the sheet furiously, finally pulling it

away from his eyes.

"Who are you?" he asked the figure ducked into the shadows before him.

"Detective O'Brien."

"There's still a woman in there," Dan whispered.

"My partner's in there with them. We'll get her."

-

Ransom heard the gunshots and braced himself for the sounds of screaming, but nothing came. As soon as the shots erupted -- along with the sounds of running and pursuit -- they stopped. Hopefully no one had been hit. Or maybe they had, but they'd been killed instantly, no time to cry out in pain before they went down.

Don't think that way.

Had any of those shots come from O'Brien? It hadn't sounded like his partner's firearm of choice. David favored one of those Dirty Harry numbers with the booming report that accompanied each shot. This had sounded more like one of those trendy numbers with the magazines chock full of rounds.

One thing was certain, whoever *was* over there, there was no one where Brick was now, which meant the field of possible locations for the others to be hiding was much too narrow. He'd need to lure someone over this way if he wanted to do his part to catch this son of a bitch.

Ransom looked around the dusty walkway and picked up an old clay brick, with all but one of its corners weathered away. He hoisted it in his free hand, weighed its heft in his palm...

Seemed appropriate somehow...

...and pitched it across the gallery, where it smashed

down on top of a metal roof.

Gunshots rang out immediately. Then the room grew quiet.

The sounds of a self-playing piano and Orson Welles' slurred voice rumbled around them.

"You hear that?" Welles mumbled. *"An echo…"*

Brick's ears tracked the sounds of running feet as his eyes scanned the metal fence that ran through this section of the gallery. The shadow of a pumpjack raced across the fence, playing tricks on his eyes. He wasn't sure if he was seeing the movement of a person, or the shadows from this bizarre gallery installation.

"Brick!" O'Brien's voice rang out from the distance. "I've got Buckley!"

Just two of 'em left. Julie and Baxter.

Brick was here.

Julie was curled up in as tight a ball as possible. The sounds from whatever had hit the roof above her had scared the ever-loving shit out of her, and the resulting gunfire and running feet had done their best to send her heart racing, almost to the point of failure. But hearing that name sent a fleeting wave of relief through her body.

Then she heard a movement over her shoulder, and a hand swept around behind her and clamped down over her mouth. At the same time, something cold and metal dug into her ribs. *Hard.*

"Don't make a move until I tell you," Baxter hissed into her ear as he pulled her swiftly to her feet. "What's your name?"

She swallowed as he released his grip over her mouth and

she tried to catch her breath. "Julie," she managed to croak out.

Baxter half-led, half-dragged her out of the shack.

"I've got Julie here!" He shouted. "Unless you want a dead woman on your hands, hold your fire."

Brick froze.

He was no more than twenty feet away, his back pressed flat against a metal drum. From here, he could easily have taken the guy out, that is, if Zack Baxter hadn't gone off and dragged someone Ransom cared about into this.

He held his breath, every possible scenario playing out in his mind.

"Let me out of here, and I'll let her go!" Baxter shouted again.

The words echoed, as a shot rang out on screen. Brick jolted at the sound, and heard the shuffling of feet again as Baxter reacted to the movie's soundtrack and started moving.

"I'm walking out of here with the girl. Hold your fire, and I'll let her go once I'm out on the street."

Should he try for a cowboy move? Try to take Baxter out before he could shoot her?

Ransom shook his head in frustration. That kind of shit only worked in the movies.

Another gunshot echoed throughout the gallery as Welles' partner shot him dead on screen.

"We're heading for the second-floor balcony. Do *not* interfere or I'm shooting Julie here in the side of the head!"

They'd moved far enough away now that Brick chanced following them. He stepped as deliberately as possible, setting his feet down one after the other, silent as a ghost, as he saw

Baxter and Julie emerge from the shadows up ahead and continue toward the exit at the far end of the room. By now, Hank Quinlan was floating facedown in a filthy river of garbage on the screen overhead. Baxter, pressing a gun into Julie's side, was walking swiftly now, looking from side to side as he shoved his hostage forward.

It took every bit of determination Ransom could muster not to haul off and risk shooting this son of a bitch in the back of his head. Instead, he kept his distance until they had slipped out of the gallery, then Brick took off running after them. He stopped at the doorway to the main balcony on the second floor. Just past the railing, Brick could see the flashing lights and neon tubes coming from the cars hanging over the open, two-story lobby below. Red and blue police lights were streaming in from the street outside, reflecting and revolving over the hundreds of thick black coils of film streaming down around the somersaulting, suspended cars. Brick peered around the corner just as Baxter spun around and caught sight of him. He immediately moved the gun away from Julie's ribs and up to her head.

"Don't fucking try it!" Baxter shouted. "Step out and place your gun on the floor!"

Julie stared back at Brick. Clearly terrified.

Not worth the risk.

Brick threw him arms out to the sides, crouched on one knee, and set his gun on the marble floor. He immediately stood up straight and stepped forward. His heart froze in his chest as he watched Baxter shuffling backward, glancing behind him every so often as he and Julie got closer to the escalators.

"I get downstairs, and I get outside, then I turn the girl

loose! *Got it?!*"

Brick nodded in understanding.

But something about that promise didn't quite add up.

Baxter had already killed at least four people. D.J. Norman. Peter Cornelius. Two members of the Greenwood Mystery Writers Circle. Yet now he claimed he'd be letting this woman go as soon as he was outside? It seemed unlikely.

Brick took a step forward.

"Keep your distance!" Baxter muttered.

Brick watched the guy's expression.

If someone was gonna get shot, he'd rather it was him than Julie.

The gun wavered in Baxter's bandaged hand, slipping forward, away from Julie's temple.

Brick took another step forward.

"I said *don't fucking move...* You hear me?" Baxter's voice was quivering now as the gun moved still farther in Brick's direction.

Ransom raised his hands higher. "I hear you."

Baxter cocked his head slightly, beads of sweat appearing on his brow.

Brick held a moment longer, then he took another step forward.

The gun swooped down from Julie's head as Baxter swept his arm forward and fired off a shot. It missed, but the noise was immediately broken by the sounds of two more shots.

Brick's head whipped to the side, where he saw O'Brien stepping out from around the corner, his smoking Dirty Harry-special held out in front of him.

Baxter screamed in pain as a plume of red erupted where O'Brien's first bullet had ripped through his already damaged hand. The gun flew free. The second bullet tore into Baxter's shoulder, and he instinctively threw his bloody hand over the wound, only to howl in pain as he unthinkingly smashed the two gunshot wounds together.

Julie scrambled to get away from him, but Baxter's other hand reached out and grabbed her by her hair. Even as he pulled her back, his good hand was going for the back of his belt, where he grabbed something and pulled it forward-

Brick started running in a full sprint, rifling through his mental catalogue of ancient football plays. Been a while since he'd used any of his Roosevelt High moves, but if he tucked his head and lowered his shoulder it just might work!

Baxter's arm was still swinging forward, bringing something with it that glimmered in the red and blue lights-

Brick watched as the knife blade appeared out of nowhere and swooped up towards Julie's neck. He swept past her, past Baxter's outstretched, bloody hand, and *slammed* into the young man's sternum with every ounce of force he could muster. He heard Baxter's breath get knocked clean out of the son of a bitch's lungs, and still he powered through with all his strength, driving the guy away from Julie and into the railing. The knife clattered to the floor as Baxter hit the guardrail with an ungodly amount of momentum and flipped backwards, over the railing and out of sight.

Brick grabbed for the metal rail, struggling to get ahold of it as he slumped breathlessly to the floor.

O'Brien ran forward in pursuit, stopping short as he glanced over the edge and recoiled in horror.

Ransom looked up at his partner. It was a one-story fall; the guy had to have survived it.

O'Brien turned around slowly, his face drooping in

disbelief.

Off to the right, a team of police officers came charging up the escalators. Brick turned in dazed confusion as he saw Anne and her forensics team walking slowly toward them.

"Ransom, have you *ever* had a case where the suspect lived long enough to go to trial?" O'Brien asked.

Brick looked at him questioningly and got to his feet. He peered down over the railing, where he saw something sweeping back and forth in a pendulum motion in the lobby below. It took him a moment to realize what had happened, but when the figure twisted around at the bottom, he saw Zack Baxter's lifeless expression looking back at him. In the fall, he had somehow managed to become tangled in the coils of heavy black film suspended from the ceiling, and the drop, along with the force of his own body weight, had apparently snapped his neck at the bottom of his descent.

Brick stumbled backward, shielding Julie's eyes as a crowd of police officers and EMTs swarmed around them. Julie threw her arms around Brick's neck and buried her face in his chest.

"It's all right, "Brick said as he tried not to look at Baxter's face. "It's all right."

<u>Six Months Later</u>

They had spent the entire day moving Julie's things into Brick's apartment at The Dean, which certainly wasn't a bad way to pass the time, especially under the circumstances, but it had taken much longer than they had expected. The weather was hot, especially for Seattle, which had made the process easier but also a whole lot sweatier. By the time they'd showered and taken a brief nap, allowing for a short but extraordinarily pleasant... *celebration* as the sun began to ease down toward the horizon, Brick realized they were very short on time before Flynn and Morgan were due for dinner. He'd thrown on some clothes and run over to Greenwood Market, while Julie stayed behind and did her best to clear up the kitchen and find some dishes.

Brick returned ten minutes later to find Flynn's car parked in front of the building. He headed up the stairs with his bag of groceries and headed inside. From the front hall he could hear Julie and Morgan chatting around the corner in the kitchen. When he stepped into the living room, Flynn was just stepping out of the bedroom, where he'd set a bassinet on the floor and was tucking its little passenger in. Brick peeked over his friend's shoulder and smiled at the peaceful little face peering out from a bundle of blankets.

"That is one *cute* kid," Brick said.

Flynn glanced over his shoulder, then turned back to his sleeping daughter. "You hear that Evie? Uncle Brick says you're beautiful."

Evie was sound asleep, so Flynn got up and quietly closed the door behind them.

"She fell asleep in the car and didn't even wake up when

we brought her inside. There's a very good chance she'll sleep through the entire movie."

"Congratulations again," Brick said as he led the way toward the kitchen.

"Thank you. Congrats to you two as well. Now, if you don't mind, Daddy needs a drink."

"Whatever you want. I'll fix you a cocktail and throw dinner together before the show. Any interest in a round of Manhattans?"

"Honestly, and keep your Freudian wisecracks out of this, but I wouldn't mind one of those shameless mother's milk concoctions of yours," Flynn said.

"OK then," Brick replied as he grabbed the Kahlua and vodka from the liquor cabinet, "but just so you know, I'm trying to salvage what remains of my masculinity, so ix-nay on the whole 'mother's milk' thing if you don't mind."

"Oh God," Julie replied as she rounded the corner and put her arm around Brick's shoulder. "You can call it whatever you like. Between the ramekin collections and the library of Jean-Claude Renoir cookbooks, my preconceived notions are getting reshuffled by the day."

"I think after what you two went through, there's no question Brick Ransom is a real man," Morgan said from the far end of the kitchen where she was leaning against the cabinets.

"Thank you!" Brick said as he set to work making a couple of White Russians for himself and Flynn.

Julie poured two glasses of rosé and handed one of them to Morgan, who closed her eyes as she swallowed a sip. *"God I missed wine."*

"Did you see our little visitor?" Julie asked.

"I did. She'd seemed right at home," Ransom replied as he topped the drinks off with a splash of cream and handed one of the glasses to Flynn.

"Speaking of which, Congratulations to the new roommates," Morgan said as she raised her wine.

"I beat you too it already," Flynn said.

The four of them clinked glasses.

"You guys get all the credit," Brick said. "Now, why don't you go into the other room and relax while I throw dinner together."

Their guests murmured their thanks as Julie led them out of the kitchen, carrying a tray of meats and cheeses to lure them to the dining table.

In the kitchen, Brick put on a pot of hot water, which he brought to a boil as he rinsed a pound of asparagus and chopped it up into one-inch pieces. He cooked a massive portion of spaghetti until it was just a minute away from tender, and threw the asparagus into the roiling water for the last minute. He drained the pasta, tossed it in the pot with a few tablespoons of butter and a bit of the pasta water, then sprinkled the whole mixture with fresh grated parmesan. In a separate pan he scrambled a large batch of eggs. Then he put a heavy scoop of noodles on each of four plates, topped each with a generous helping of eggs, finished that off with a dollop of ricotta, and topped it all off with a sprinkling of salt and fresh pepper.

He brought the plates into the dining room and was met by a trio of spinning heads.

"My God that was fast," Morgan exclaimed.

"Figured you guys were hungry. I know we are," Brick said as he spread out the plates and joined them at the table.

"Brick is teaching me a bit about cooking," Julie said. "And in exchange I'm giving him a little introduction to film noir."

Julie gave Brick a little knowing wink. "Noir" had become a codeword of sorts since their first night together.

Flynn noticed the exchange but decided to let it pass without ribbing. When two of your good friends wound up moving in together, you didn't give them a hard time.

"So, what's the movie of choice for tonight?"

"'Kiss Me Deadly,'" Julie replied. "One of the all-time greats, and unlike 'The Big Sleep,' you don't need a study guide to follow what's happening."

Flynn swallowed a bit, hesitated, and set down his fork. "Speaking of which, I'm hoping enough time has gone by that you don't mind my asking, but what exactly happened with that whole D.J. Norman/Dan Buckley debacle?"

Brick took a sip of his drink and glanced at Julie. She seemed to have taken the whole thing more or less in stride after the initial exhaustion that followed such an emotional event, but whenever the subject came up, he always sized up her reaction, just to be sure it wouldn't upset her.

As usual, she was tough as nails.

"Basically, Zack Baxter was your typical wound-up fanatic. At one time he'd been friendly with Buckley, even found himself in the inner circle of sorts when he worked for his publisher and *briefly* worked on the revisions of one of his books. But it wasn't long before he got a bit too territorial for comfort and Maureen Alexander let him go."

"But how did he end up killing Diane Norman and those other folks?" Morgan asked. "Why did he even do it?"

"Like I said, he was a fanatic. He took Dan Buckley's

success as representing a bit of his own self-worth. He came from a wealthy family, had relatives back in Colorado footing the bills for him, even if they didn't exactly encourage him to come home for holiday visits. So, he was isolated out here, out of work, and he sort of saw Buckley's success as mirroring his own, even if he felt his friend was beginning to squander his talents. When Diane Norman and Peter Cornelius started bad-mouthing Buckley's work, Baxter took it personally. *Extremely personally,* to the point that he decided anyone who publicly lambasted Buckley's books was a traitor and had to be removed from the equation."

"But what about the museum? What was he after there?" Flynn interjected.

Brick took a sip of his White Russian, then began, "I think Beverly Pepper's power and money scared him. She made a few ill-advised comments to the press about taking Dan Buckley's attention away from his work, gave the impression she'd make him a kept man, and in the process, maybe his work would have to fall by the wayside as well."

"And knowing someone like Baxter – who himself depended on financial support from his family in Colorado – that made her an extremely dangerous woman to have around, so far as he was concerned," Julie added now.

"So he showed up at Noir City aiming to kill Beverly Pepper, or even take out Dan Buckley if need be," Brick looked Julie in the eyes for a moment. "In the end, when that didn't happen, he was just out to spill any blood he could. But in *his mind,* so far as I can guess, everything he was doing was an attempt to somehow preserve the publishing legacy of Daniel Buckley, or warp it in his own way, even if it meant cutting off the supply of his drug of choice."

"The books?" Flynn asked hesitantly.

"The books."

"So long story short, the guy was a fucking nutcase," Julie concluded.

They sat quietly for a moment.

"Well," Morgan said finally. "Maybe I've become a lightweight over the past ten months and this is the wine talking, but I for one am glad the son of a bitch is dead."

Julie nodded her head quietly.

"It certainly could have ended up a whole lot worse," Brick said.

"Yes it could have," Flynn said. "Thank God it didn't. Now, on a happier note, when do we start the movie?"

Julie got up and walked across the room to the TV, where she picked up the evening's selection, then walked back and set it before Flynn.

"Anytime you're ready. One of the ultimate film noir classics."

Brick got up and slipped into the kitchen. "Anyone else want another drink?"

"I'm good," Flynn said.

"Me too," Morgan replied as she sipped her drink and looked at the back of the movie case in her husband's hand.

"You can't hang up the meat hook?!" She read aloud in disgust.

"I might have a little more wine," Julie said.

She got up and headed into the kitchen, where she slipped up behind Brick, putting her arms around him and hugging him close as she kissed him on the back of the neck, just behind his ear.

"You ready for the movie?"

Michael Attebery

"As ready as I'll ever be," Brick said
"Be sure to watch for those dark deeds in the shadows,"
Julie whispered. "There will be a test later."

Acknowledgments

Thanks once again to Jason Croatto for the great cover art and interior layout!

Thanks to Elizabeth Attebery for her assistance in preparing this book for publication.

I can't forget the help of my editorial assistants, Winter and Mocha, who have provided welcome entertainment and amusement as I've poured over the text of this book.

Thanks to my friends for their support of my writing over all these years.

And of course, immeasurable thanks my wife Stephanie, who has put up with me for 14 years now, and has read the early drafts of every one of my books. I couldn't do any of this without your patience and support…

Mike Attebery earned a Bachelor of Fine Arts Degree from the School of Film and Animation at the Rochester Institute of Technology. When he isn't writing or editing books and film reviews, Mike spends his days kicking and knocking on stuff to see what it's made out of. He lives in Seattle, Washington with his wife and daughter, and their ferrets, Winter and Mocha. He is currently at work on his fifth novel.

www.mikeattebery.com